Mills & Boon
Best Seller Romance

A chance to read and collect some of the best-loved novels from Mills & Boon—the world's largest publisher of romantic fiction.

Every month, four titles by favourite Mills & Boon authors will be re-published in the *Best Seller Romance* series.

A list of other titles in the *Best Seller Romance* series can be found at the end of this book.

Violet Winspear

THE SIN
OF CYNARA

MILLS & BOON LIMITED
LONDON · TORONTO

CHAPTER ONE

THE train sped on through the darkness with a swift monotony, and every few miles it swept around the bends with a breathless roar, tearing away at the miles like some great beast of the night.

Although Carol felt apprehensive about this journey she was making, she felt sure she had made the right decision with regard to Teri. He belonged in Italy with his own sort of people and it was up to her to take him to Falconetti.

Her preparations had been made secretly and carefully, so as to avoid arguments with the Aunts until the very last moment. Carol couldn't have faced the tantrums and the tears, having had a feast of trouble since her sister Cynara had run off and left her to cope on her own.

The Aunts owned and ran the Copper Jug, a tea-room in the centre of the high street of Chalkleigh, a sea-country town with an outwardly serene air; a place that held the view that so long as grubby linen wasn't aired in public it was all right to pretend that it didn't exist.

It would have been insupportable for the Aunts if their cosy clients, who came to the tea-room to enjoy buttered scones and strawberry tarts with a really hot pot of tea, had ever learned that the child Teri had been born to Cynara, who after his birth had vanished from the hospital and left him to be-brought home to Chalkleigh by Carol, to be passed off as her son.

After all, her husband had been his father ... Vincenzo, whom she had married after a whirlwind courtship, only to find him on the very day of the wedding making love to her sister.

Carol had never lived with Vincenzo in the real sense of the word, agreeing not to make scandal for the Aunts by insisting on a divorce from the handsome Italian who had promised so ardently to make her happy and had given her disillusion in its place.

'Why didn't you marry Cynara?' she demanded of him.

'Because I didn't have to.' He hadn't said it brutally, but with the reasonable air of a Latin who would never have dreamed of marrying any girl but a virgin. That was part of his creed ... and it was part of Carol's nature to become icily indifferent to anyone who broke her trust in them, without even a touch of guilt to soften the painful blow. With an infuriating lack of principle Vincenzo had thought he could possess both the Adams sisters, and had swiftly learned that Carol didn't play those kind of games.

He had made her despise him, right up until the day he had died. He and Cynara had been at a funfair when the roller-coaster had gone off the rails and a number of people had been flung from the whirling cars. Carol's sister had been hurt, but Vincenzo had been killed instantly and there hadn't been a mark on his dark, chiselled face that had fooled Carol into thinking him as fine as he looked. But his looks had been a perfect mask, and she had no more time for Italian men, and was only concerned that Teri wouldn't grow up to be as unprincipled as his charming Casanova of a father.

Teri was now five years old, and what had precipitated Carol's decision to take him to Italy had been the letter she had received from her sister, far away in Texas and now married to an executive there ... alarmed that her husband would find out about the child, Cynara had begged Carol to go on pretending to be his mother.

In lots of ways Carol didn't have to pretend. Teri believed her to be his true mother and she had never disillusioned him. Nor had the Aunts ever breathed a word to the contrary. They wanted people to believe that he was the legal child of their niece Carol ... the grubby linen of her unhappy marriage had been tucked away by them, and they, like Cynara, didn't want it disturbed.

The marriage and its sad end was a dark crucible from which Carol had emerged heart-cool and never again to be the young dreamer of gallant knights who came along and swept a girl off her feet. She had believed in love, but her experience had taught her that other people were only concerned to find pleasure where they could and to the devil with the heartache they caused. She had grown cynical, and the only emotion she now valued was what she felt for Teri.

He had the right to have things that boys with fathers had, and she just hadn't the means to provide

7

them. Since Cynara had run away and left the Aunts without a waitress, she had quit her own job as a library book-restorer and taken over from her sister at the tea-room. Which meant that she had board and lodging but a very low wage.

She just couldn't see a way to educate and care for Teri without assistance from Vincenzo's family, and she was desperately tired of being run off her feet for a mere pittance, for ever at the beck and call of the Aunts.

Little old ladies, but bittersweet tyrants who felt she owed them her energy and her loyalty because they had taken care of Cynara and herself when their mother had died and their father had gone off to Central America to work. Out there he had married a Brazilian widow with a family of her own, and the twin sisters in England had found themselves dependent on the Aunts.

Dependency had a sting to it, as Carol had learned, but she owed it to Teri to see that his father's people met him and made some sort of provision for his future. He was a quick, bright, affectionate child, and certain things about Vincenzo had informed her that he didn't come from one of the poorer families of southern Italy. He had always had ample pocket money and good suits to wear, and Teri wasn't going to have a deprived boyhood if she could help it. He existed because of Vincenzo, and she had made up her mind that if the Falcone family was a comfortable one, then the boy was going to share in that comfort.

She didn't intend to ask anything for herself, but she

fully meant to go on playing the part to which Cynara's sin had consigned her. To the Falcones she would present herself as Teri's mother, and there would be no one, least of all his real mother, to say that she told a lie.

She gave her pillow another thump and tucked the blanket closer about her legs. This was the first time she had travelled all night on a train, and her limited means had not made it possible for her to afford first-class accommodation. The compartment felt rather cold, but Teri was well wrapped up and sound asleep, and somehow she hadn't expected to sleep easily herself. Her parting from the Aunts was still like the sting from a deep scratch.

'Don't come running back to us when that Italian lot throw you out,' Aunt Lottie had shrilled at her. 'We'll get another waitress, and there won't be any more room for you and that mischievous little dago. Do you really imagine that these people are going to take you in and provide for you – *his* relatives, that foreigner with the morals of a tomcat? You'll be sorry all round, my girl, giving up a good home here to go off to this place with the outlandish name.'.

'Falconetti,' she had told her aunt, holding firmly to her patience and her decision to seek a better life for Teri. 'It's an *isola* off the Lake of Lina, and though I'd be the last person to pretend that Vincenzo treated me fairly, the boy has Falcone blood in his veins and even if they turn me away from their door, they won't do it to Teri. On my own I just can't give him the things he should have; on the wage I earn here I can barely

9

afford to buy his clothes now he's springing up so quickly.'

'You get your food, the pair of you, and a decent bed,' Aunt Rachel had broken in, less shrill than her sister but with something more deadly in her eyes. '*They* won't want you, no more than he did. There was always something a bit too proud about you, my girl, and let me remind you that if it hadn't been for *our* generosity you and that man-crazy sister of yours would have been packed off to an institution.'

'I daresay we would,' Carol agreed, 'and you, dear aunts, would have lost a pair of underpaid servants. Half Cynara's trouble was that she wanted a bit of life after being on her feet all day, dashing about with trays, and listening to the snobbish gossip of the women who come to the Copper Jug to eat cream cakes – cats, some of them, ridiculously jealous of a girl like Cynara because she always outshone their own daughters for looks. I don't condone what she did, nor do I applaud Vincenzo. But I'm going to see to it that Teri grows up in a different environment.'

And Carol meant it. Even if the Falcones didn't want her as part of their ménage, then she would find the courage from somewhere to leave the boy in their keeping. Italians were kind to children, whereas at the Copper Jug he was in everlasting hot water with the Aunts. Like any child he had big eyes for creamy cakes and it had been difficult keeping him away from them. They were Aunt Rachel's speciality, and more than once she had cuffed Teri and called him a sneaking little thief, merely because his childish tummy couldn't resist a sticky strawberry tart.

Falconetti sounded a wild and countrified place, and was probably a large farm of the Sabine variety. Vincenzo hadn't talked a great deal of his family, but there had been no doubt that he had been well educated and rather spoiled.

It worried her a little that Teri might be spoiled, but on the other hand he could be deprived and brought up in fear of a pair of elderly women who had never known love themselves and clutched to their bosoms instead a Victorian code of morality and a fondness for the pennies they rarely gave away.

It had been a difficult decision for Carol to make, especially about a child who wasn't really hers. She had thought of writing to the Falcone family, and had then decided that it might come as a more delightful surprise if they were suddenly confronted by the boy, who most certainly resembled his father.

She had once asked Vincenzo why he had left Italy to come and work (if that was the correct word) in London. He had replied that he wanted to see more of the world . . . and Carol had learned the hard way that he really meant that he wanted to sample the kind of girls who liked a good time and were less careful of their virginity if they were not Latin born.

Poor Vincenzo . . . whatever his faults he hadn't deserved to die so young.

Carol drifted off to sleep, and awoke to pale light drifting into the railway compartment, and a crick in her neck. Teri had climbed out of his nest of blankets and was at the window with his nose pressed to the glass.

'Are we in Italy, Cally?'

That was his special name for her. 'When do we go on the boat – directly we get off the train?'

'Not quite, Buster.' That was her special name for him. 'We get off at a place called Catalina, where we'll have something to eat, and then we take a cab to the lakeside and that's where we hire the boat.'

Teri turned from the window to grin at her, his great dark eyes fixed lovingly upon her face. 'Isn't it a lovely holiday, Cally? I liked sleeping on a train all night, did you?'

'Ever so much,' she said wryly, emerging from her own blanket and stretching her slim legs. 'I think we'll go and wash up, *caro*, and make ourselves more presentable.'

She held out a hand to him, and with her overnight bag clutched in her other hand they made their way to the washroom, already occupied by a stout and smiling Italian woman who at once made room for them at the wash-basin.

She chattered away to Teri, obviously recognizing him for an Italian child, and because Carol had taken endless trouble to teach him his father's language (which she had learned partly from Vincenzo and from a course at evening classes) the boy was able to reply to the woman's questions.

He told her all about their day in Rome, which Carol had also enjoyed, though conscious all the time that she wasn't really in Italy to fall in love with the warm sun, the jostling old houses, and the *dolce far niente* attitude of mind. She held on to her emotions

12

just in case she wasn't wanted here, but couldn't deprive Teri of a walk through the gardens of the Palace of the Caesars, with its evocative ruins and wild-flowering shrubs; its crazy-paved paths and the perpetual husky music of the cicadas, Aesop's feckless fiddlers.

At the Fontana di Trevi, with its water-gods and stone horses pawing the air, and the cascades beneath which the rock nymphs shone in the water, she and Teri threw pennies into the basin and made their wishes.

Hers was simply that the Falcone family would accept Teri and take him to their hearts.

They drove in a *carrozza* to the railway station, and now they were almost at their destination . . . the Lake of Lina.

'*Ah, Roma, non basta una vita,*' said the Italian woman, with a blissful smile.

Rome, a lifetime is not enough! Probably not, thought Carol, and she didn't dare hope that Italy was going to be her place of residence. Teri belonged here because of his father, but she had been a wife in name only, and was a mother in name only.

'Be always a good boy to your mother.' The Italian woman patted Teri's cheek. 'You are going to be a handsome *cavaliere* when you grow up, with all the girls after you, but never forget your very first girl, the one who loves you best of all – *una bionda bella.*'

When the woman had gone from the wash-room, Teri gazed up at Carol, watching her as she combed her hair. 'Are you the blonde girl, Cally?' he asked her.

13

'I have fair hair,' she smiled. 'That is what the lady meant.'

'Then why is mine dark?' he wanted to know, turning to the wall mirror to stare at his own mop of brunette hair.

'Because you take after your father, Buster. He was dark, like most Italian men.'

'Was he nice?' This was a question Teri had asked her more than once, and it troubled her and made her wonder if he had overheard anything the Aunts might have said about Vincenzo.

She thought of the Vincenzo she had fallen in love with, thinking him so much more gallant and charming than the rather intellectual young men who came in and out of the town library where she worked.

'Yes, he had some nice ways,' she told his young son. 'He could be very charming.'

But he could also be weak and reckless, and she couldn't bear to think of Teri growing up to follow in his father's footsteps. He was all she had in the world to love and she wanted him to be a fine, strong, good man.

They were now in Sabine country, with its olive farms and flocks of sheep in the hills. Here in this unspoiled place there might be a place for Teri and he might take to it more than his father had. After all, he had a dash of Adams blood in his veins, which might dilute those Latin passions.

When the train drew into the station, they were among the few people to alight. A young porter came running to take their cases, and Carol asked him if there was a nearby café where some breakfast could be had.

'*Si, signora.*' He good-naturedly lugged the cases all the way out of the station to the café itself, where the tables were already set out on the pavement, with tubs of oleanders near the entrance. 'We're going to Falconetti,' Carol told the porter. 'Do you know the place?'

'*Si, palàgio del isola.*' He smiled, accepted his tip, and left Carol feeling stunned.

The palace on the island! Oh, he had to be mistaken, or was kidding her. At no time had Vincenzo led her to believe that his family was of the *aristocrazia*, but suddenly she felt a quickening of her nerves and wondered at her own audacity in coming all this way to confront them with the child ... if they were important, then it would look as if she were trying to cash in on their good fortune.

And yet why not? There was no disputing the fact that Teri was of their blood, and she wanted nothing for herself. Her marriage to Vincenzo had died before it had begun to live, and what love she now had to give had been transferred to the child which Cynara's affair with her husband had brought into the world.

'Come along, Buster, sit down at the table and we'll have something nice to eat.'

His attention was on the doves that strutted around the tables searching for crumbs, but at the mention of food he came and scrambled on to a chair. 'Ice-cream,' he said, with a coaxing smile, 'with chocolate sauce?'

'Not for breakfast, *caro*.' And when the waiter came out to them she asked if they could have one coffee, one glass of warm sweet milk, soft-boiled eggs, bread, butter and marmalade.

Si, they could have all that, and something called *marmellata* which was made by the monks out of figs and apricots. '*E bella!*' he assured her, and he stared at her with bold eyes, for the sun was playing over her blonde hair, braided at the crown of her head and revealing the slim whiteness of her neck where a little silver coin rested on a chain in the pool of her throat. Her dress was of white and grey, and it made her look as sedate as a young novice.

But cool as she outwardly looked Carol hadn't forgotten how disturbing the eyes of Italian men could be, for there was no shyness or constraint in the way they looked at a woman.

Carol hadn't bothered in the past five years to have anything to do with men and had devoted herself to Teri. Consequently she had almost forgotten that her combination of very fair hair and grey-violet eyes could have a certain effect on men who were totally opposite in colouring – the last man to tell her she was attractive was Vincenzo, and she had coldly replied that he no longer had the power to turn her head with his Latin flattery.

But she wasn't the only one to notice the waiter's preoccupation with her hair. 'She's my mummy!' Teri suddenly cried out, and jumping off his chair he ran round to Carol and buried his face against her, hugging her with fierce young arms.

'What a big *bambino*,' the waiter scoffed, and quirking an eyebrow at Carol he strolled off into the café to fetch their breakfast.

'Now don't be silly, Buster.' Carol kissed the top of Teri's head. 'We're going to have eggs and soldiers, and you like those.'

'That man was looking all over you.' Teri pouted, unaccustomed to men because they very rarely came into the Copper Jug, and already precocious enough to recognize the light of admiration in a rival's eye. He lifted a hand and stroked her hair, which he alone knew was incredibly long and shining when let down out of the thick braids. It came past the curve of Carol's spine, and was her only true vanity. Both she and Cynara had the same hair, but her sister cut hers long ago and wore it in a glossy pageboy style. But there was an element of the old-fashioned girl in Carol and she liked having long hair. Teri loved it and would sometimes brush it for her, and call it her serpent's tail, curling it around her slender body with husky giggles.

There was a shadow of doubt in Teri's heart and mind that she was his 'mummy', and there were times when Carol grew frightened in case he ever learned the truth.

'Come on, be my big man and sit down to have your breakfast. We can't be here all day, remember. We have to get that boat, *caro*.'

'The boat!' He clapped his hands with anticipation, for boats were one of his passions. Then, after planting a kiss on Carol's neck, he returned to his seat and grinned across the table at her. Such huge eyes, she thought, fringed by lashes exactly like his father's. She sighed deep in her heart ... how different life could have been if Vincenzo had lived up to his promises and her hopes. Instead he had ruined her dreams with all the carelessness of a selfish, half-grown boy, and in so doing he had broken himself on the wheel of pleasure.

'Don't look sad, Cally!'

She smiled at Teri, the son of her virginal marriage. 'I'm just a bit anxious, *caro*. I hope your daddy's people like us.'

'If they don't, Cally, then we'll go to Rome and live there, near the fountain of King Neptune.' He had very much taken to the bearded old god in the Fountain of Trevi, with his trident and his chariot.

'That would be nice,' she said, and wondered if it would also be possible. Her small store of cash was almost exhausted, but one thing in her favour was that she could speak good Italian and had a good experience of working as a waitress. There were plenty of cafés in Rome, and no doubt plenty of cheap rooms.

Yet ... oh, it wasn't what she wanted for Teri. Living from hand to mouth, making do with mended clothes, and never being able to send him to a really good school. Education was so important for a boy, especially one as bright and quick as her little Roman.

She smiled at him, and hers was a singularly sweet smile for anyone she cared for. 'We'll keep our fingers crossed, *caro*. Wouldn't you like to live on a real *isola*, among your own kind of people?'

He nodded and played with his spoon. 'I shall miss Auntie's fruit tarts,' he said.

'Yes,' she said wryly, and remembered all those times

18

her aunt had stormed at the boy for poking about in her kitchen and nipping hot tarts off the table.

Their breakfast arrived and they tucked into the food with good appetite. Their journey to Catalina had been rather a long one, and for the most part they had lived on cheese sandwiches and biscuits. Teri's eggs were nice and runny so he could dip his soldiered bread into the golden yolks. Carol sipped her real Italian coffee with appreciation, and thoroughly enjoyed the fig and apricot jam on crusty bread.

When the waiter made out their bill, she asked him if there was a local bus to the Lake of Lina, for it would work out a little cheaper to go that way instead of hiring a car. 'Si,' he gave her a bold smile and told her they would be in time to pick up the bus in the nearby square. 'Is the *signora* taking a holiday in this part of the world?'

'We're on a visit to relatives,' she said, counting coins into his palm. 'That was a very nice breakfast, *grazie*.'

'It has been a pleasure serving you, *signora*.' He gave her a gallant bow, while Teri tugged at her hand and glared at the man for having the nerve to flirt with his Cally.

'Your luggage, *signora*, I will get the kitchen boy to carry the cases to the bus for you.'

'That's kind of you.'

'Who would not be kind to a young mother and her *bambino*?' He winked at Teri, and went off to find the kitchen boy, and Carol wondered if she was going to find the same sort of kindness at the house of the Falcone family . . . the palace on the island. Oh, it had to be an exaggeration of the porter, who probably regarded any large house as a *palazzo*.

The dusty, old-fashioned bus was already being revved up for its journey when they arrived in the square. Her cases were hoisted aboard and she and the boy found seats about half-way along the bus. The other passengers gave them long stares of curiosity, and she heard a woman mutter something to another one. These were real country people, with sunburned faces and dark shawls and wide-brimmed hats to offset the rising heat of the Italian sun . . . the *solleone*, merciless sunlion of late summer.

The bus started up and bumped its way out of the *piazza*, passed the huddling, colour-washed houses and shops and roared merrily over a hump-backed bridge on to a road bordered by sword-leaved cacti, sharply duelling with each other, their sharp points glittering.

That woman on the other side of the aisle had turned her head and was staring at Teri with sharp eyes. He moved closer to Carol and his hand gripped hers. That look from one of the locals couldn't be malignant, for the child was too obviously Italian; it could only mean that his looks were recognizable and he resembled the Falcone family. Right away Carol wanted to ask someone about them, but when she glanced around for a sympathetic face she found that unsmiling curiosity of villagers who regarded all strangers as intruders into their close-knit lives. They could see that the boy was one of them, but she wasn't and therefore was a source of suspicion and unrest. When she caught their gaze they glanced away from her and made her realize how wide a gulf she had to cross in order to become acceptable to them.

Oh dear, would it be the same with the Falcones? Must she really face the wrenching pain of having to part with Teri in order to ensure for him a secure future?

She glanced down at his dark head and couldn't bear to think of being without him, yet that probability loomed very near. That these Sabine people didn't welcome strangers was very evident, and she could only suppose that the friendly waiter at the café came from Rome where the people were far more sophisticated.

Teri gave her a quick smile and she forced the pensive look from her face and shared his interest in the passing scenery. Farmhouses spread across the sunlit hills, with massive wooden gates and groves of chestnut trees. The road lifted and fell and curved around the Sabine farms, and she marvelled at the timeless beauty of it all. These fortress-like farms and olive terraces had been like this in the time of the Roman occupation; they had built the triple-arched bridges and marched in their legions along this very road.

It was exciting and she couldn't help but respond to the antiquity of the countryside and the fabulous history. Here the soldiers had carried off the Sabine women and their screams had echoed through these hills, and their petticoats of blue or pea-green would have billowed across the saddlebows of their rough and laughing abductors. Would it have been so terrible, she wondered, to be carried off by a warrior, hard, lean

21

and campaign-scarred?

Her heart gave a tiny flutter in her breast. Was that the kind of man she really preferred, deep in her secret heart? But surely in this day and age such men were no longer existent, daring and dangerous, and riding hard across this sun-cracked land where the wild red geraniums spilled among the swords of cacti and the agaves.

They arrived suddenly at the Lake of Lina, the road twisting suddenly to give a wide and gleaming view of the lake, with its long harbour wall and rising tiers of colourful houses. The bus came to a halt in the cobbled *piazza*, and the sun struck hot as Carol and Teri climbed down the steps and were soon left on their own, their suitcases beside them, the rest of the passengers dispersing to their homes.

Stone steps led down to the shoreline of the lake and there they found a boatman who agreed to take them to the *isola*, and because Carol was so obviously a foreigner he asked a fare which she knew to be a high one. But she couldn't argue with him. Only by boat could they get to Falconetti, and having come this far they might as well go the rest of the way and discover for themselves what kind of a family she had married into.

Their cases were stowed into the boat and an excited Teri was persuaded to sit down before he fell in the lake. He chattered away to the boatman while Carol sat in silence and watched the island loom nearer at every stroke of the oars. She was approaching the Falcones with trepidation in her heart, and it grew as the boat circled the island, making for the jetty beneath waterworn walls, where on a stretch of shingle rested a few colourful sailing boats.

Her gaze slowly lifted from the jetty to where a towering, majestic house hung among a jungle of green vines, sun-burnished and sea-cooled, and exactly like the villa of a Roman governor, white-columned, open to the sun, wide-terraced, there above the water on its own great balcony of rock.

Carol caught her breath in wonder. So it was true! The house of the Falcone was a *palazzo*, and Vincenzo's family did have the means to give Teri a better life than she could.

'Look, *caro*,' she directed his attention to the proud-looking place, its walls the colour of champagne, its hanging gardens and terraces suspended as if by magic in the warm air. 'That is the house where your father was born – isn't it beautiful?'

Teri gazed at the great house with enormous eyes ... it had all the splendour of a painting in one of his story books, there on its very own island, waiting there to welcome the boy, or deny him.

'Is it real, Cally?' he asked. 'Is that where we're going to live?'

'It's real enough, *caro*, but I don't know about living there. We shall just have to wait and see how your father's people feel about us.' As their boat glided towards the jetty, she stared up at the house and told herself with some defiance that the Falcones could share some of their good fortune with Teri because they owed it to him. He was quick with life and a certain

23

beauty of face because of Vincenzo, and there had been a time when she would have had the right to come here without feeling guilty.

But she mustn't feel guilty or it might show in her eyes. For five years she had been accepted without question as Teri's mother, and there was no reason why her claim should be held in doubt by the Falcones. She didn't ask anything for herself, but it would be wonderful if she could stay here with him.

Her heart beat anxiously, and a wistful eagerness shone in her grey eyes shot with violet. Falconetti was poles from the Copper Jug and its perpetual aroma of baking cakes and pots of tea; its eternal gossip and small-town pretensions; its back-room bickering and penny-pinching by the Aunts who tucked all their profits into a building society and begrudged Teri the occasional strawberry tart.

She set her chin, with its delicate shadow of a cleft, and made up her mind to stay if she could. In fact, she very much doubted if Teri would be parted from her, for his fingers clung to hers all the way up the winding path to the scrolled gates of the house. The two bigger suitcases they left at the foot of the steps, for the stepped path was a steep one and she had a suspicion she was going to need all her breath for this confrontation with Vincenzo's family.

A strange family, who at the time of his death had sent some sort of official to collect his remains and had made no contact with her. Too hurt by too many events at the time, Carol had ignored them as they ignored her, but now she must pocket her pride.

24

'Look at those flowers, Cally.' Teri stared wonderingly at a great mass of oleander blossoms against a wall, overhung by a persimmon tree whose gold and crimson flowers were dazzling against the pale stonework. And there at the centre of the courtyard was an ornamental pool of fish flanked by tall stone vases into which masks, garlands and shells had been carved. Teri tugged his fingers free of Carol's and he ran eagerly to the pool to gaze at the darting gold fish with tails like chiffon.

Carol smiled and gazed around her. Beautiful, she thought again, as if time had stood still on this island in the sun. How could Vincenzo ever have left to go following the siren call of pleasure . . . a hedonistic fling which had ended in tragedy.

At that time Teri had been only a secret guilt on Cynara's mind, and with Vincenzo gone she had turned to Carol and begged for her help. Carol had given it . . . always a giver and never a taker.

She walked slowly towards a lovely old fountain in the shape of a nymph . . . Cyrene, perhaps, who had rebelled against Aidoneus for his tyranny and been turned to ornamental stone that would always weep, as the fountain wept its sparkling tears in the sunlight.

Suddenly Carol became aware that someone was standing in the shadow of an archway leading from another section of the large courtyard and she slowly faced around until she was looking at the person who silently watched her.

It was a young woman in a long scarlet skirt and a white silk blouse that shimmered as she came out into

25

the brightness from the shadows. Her hair was raven, like two close wings against her shapely head, and she had a wild sort of beauty and temperament in her face.

'And who might you be?' She spoke in perfect English, but with a husky accent. Then she stared at Teri, who was also staring at her. The girl gave a gasp and a hand flew to her mouth. *'Santo Dio!'* And there came into her ebony eyes such a look of frightened wonder that she might have been looking at a ghost.

'This is Terence.' Carol spoke in a quiet, steady voice, for she guessed at once that the Italian girl had recognized Vincenzo in the face of his son. 'And I am Carol Falcone – the widow of—'

'No,' the girl broke in sharply, '*I* am the widow of Vincenzo Falcone, and you are that English girl he had an affair with in England. How dare you come here? The *baróne* will kill you for daring to bring your brat to this house so we can have scandal all over again!'

Carol stood there like that stone statue of Cyrene, and her face was completely white. She made no attempt to deny the girl's statement ... she accepted it with that same icy feeling with which she had accepted Vincenzo's affair with Cynara. He had been utterly amoral, and once again she was the victim of his amorous inclinations.

'I don't want to be killed, Cally!' Teri ran to her and she drew him hard and close against her.

'No one is going to hurt a hair on your head, my son,' she said, and she tilted her chin and met the blazing eyes of the Italian beauty who had been unable to hold Vincenzo ... no one woman could ever have tamed and subdued him.

'Who is the *baróne*?' Carol asked, for she couldn't be turned away by an hysterical girl. She had to speak to someone in authority here, who could help to untangle this web in which Vincenzo had snared his women like an unscrupulous spider.

'I wouldn't advise you to speak with him,' the girl replied. 'Go back where you came from and leave us alone—'

'I'm not afraid of this man, whoever he is!' Carol said it with more assurance than she really felt. Who was he? The father of Vincenzo, and therefore the grandfather of Teri? 'He owes me a hearing for the sake of my little boy, who as you can see, *signora,* is the son of your – your dead husband. A confrontation can no longer be avoided with the *baróne*. I take it he is the head of the house?'

'Of course he is!' The girl said it with a proud, angry toss of her head. 'Are you pretending that you know nothing of Rudolph? In all probability you have come here to have an affair with him, but he can't have his head turned as easily as his brother—'

'His brother?' Carol took her up. 'Vincenzo and this man – Rudolph?'

'How innocent you pretend to be!' was the scornful reply. 'If you are hoping to worm your way into the *palazzo* with your *love child*, then you are in for a shock. You weren't wanted when Vincenzo died, and you are not wanted now, and you'd be wise to turn tail and run before you ever face Rudolph with your demands. He isn't a lover of every woman like his brother was. His

27

eyes and hands won't chase all over you, but he will chase you from off his property.

'I'll take a chance on that,' Carol rejoined. 'Do I go into the house through that archway?'

She pointed to the one from which the girl had appeared, and then holding Teri firmly by the hand she marched out of the sunlight into the shadow and stepped across a threshold into the great, mosaic-floored hall of the *palazzo*.

Across the hall a manservant in a striped waistcoat was dusting the clusters of wall-lamps and Carol went straight across to him and asked him in a firm voice to show her the way to his master. His jaw dropped and he gaped at her.

'*Andiamo!*' she said. 'If you will be so good.'

'If you will come this way, *signora*.' He led her and Teri up a curving flight of marble stairs to the *piano nobile* and there he paused in front of an imposing door and knocked upon it. Then he quickly said, '*Scuzate!*' and hurried away down the stairs, leaving Carol to obey the summons to enter the room that lay beyond the door.

'Come, Teri,' she said. 'Let's face the Lord High Executioner!'

CHAPTER TWO

IT was an immense room, looming ahead of Carol and the boy as they entered at that deep, peremptory command. Carol was aware of fine and imposing furnishings even though her attention was upon that figure seated behind a carved Renaissance desk under the high windows draped in a flame-coloured material.

Teri's fingers gripped hers and she felt a quick stab of compassion for him. It was all so strange for a little boy who had spent his life in a quiet seaside town, and she wanted to grab him fast in her arms and storm at this *baróne* that neither she nor Teri had asked to find themselves at the mercy of circumstances; both of them were the innocent victims of other people's passions.

The carpet underfoot made their progress towards the desk a silent one, and the *baróne* was seated half-turned towards the window so that Carol saw him in profile and noticed the bold Roman nose, the thick straight brow, the hollowed temple beneath the sweep of raven-black hair. Haughty, of course, and bound to be as good-looking as Vincenzo . . . and then he slowly turned in his chair and it deeply shocked her that the other side of his face had been seared as if by fire.

He stared directly into her eyes, gauging her reaction to his face and catching instantly the wave of shock that ran over her features. His lips moved, just slightly, and he rose to his feet and she was aware of a sombre elegance, and a lean, dark power of body and personality. He was a sardonic Mephisto, with a mesmeric quality to the falcon-gold eyes in that bedevilled face.

Still watching her without words he flung back the lid of an antique humidor on his desk and took from it a cigar wrapped in gold foil. His hands were lean, with the masculine beauty that must have made him overwhelming before his face had been so cruelly ruined.

The fingers of his right hand played with the cigar even as he moved his left hand to a bell on the desk. Carol could feel her nerves vibrating, but she was no cotton candy girl to be frightened by this scarred scion of Italian nobility.

'You don't have to send for a servant to throw me out, *signore*,' she said, and was glad that she had her voice under control. 'Teri and I haven't come here to beg, nor do I intend to insist that you owe him recognition as a member of your family. I merely wanted you to see him so you can judge for yourself that he is Vincenzo's son even if – if I'm not your brother's legal wife. We went through a form of marriage and I have the papers to prove it—'

'My dear madam,' the voice was like dark honey strewn with gravel, 'what are you talking about? You invade my privacy and talk in riddles. Who are you?'

'I'm the woman your brother married in England.' Temper came into Carol's eyes, with their Harlequin slant and their hint of violet in the grey, the colour of the moonstone. 'You know about me, and you can certainly see for yourself that my son resembles your brother.'

30

The falcon eyes dwelt on Teri, who looked back at the tall figure with that fearlessness which Carol had taught him. 'Children have been known to scream when they look at me.' The scarred lips moved in a twisted smile. 'Yes, I'll admit he's the living image of Vincenzo, and he seems to have his brand of effrontery. Don't I frighten you, little one?'

'You're very tall,' Teri said, conversationally. 'Are you going to smoke that gold thing?'

Carol was watching the *baróne* very closely, and she felt a strange stab of the heart as he quirked an eyebrow at the boy and seemed for a brief moment at a loss for words. Then he glanced at the cigar in his fingers and drew off the gold foil. 'Nothing is ever quite what it seems, young one,' he said, in that singular voice that held a brooding quality, its accent adding to the perfection of his English. 'One moment a sort of magic, and then the next a mere cigar.'

He struck a match and as he lit the cigar the flame was close to his face and Carol felt a shiver run through her. Yes, it had been fire which had destroyed that magnificent face, and for some sardonic reason of his own this man had never submitted to the knife of the plastic surgeon. He preferred to carry his scars, and she wondered why.

As smoke issued from the edge of his lips, the door of this emotion-charged room was opened and a young girl of about sixteen came in. She gave Carol and Teri a surprised look, and then came to the *baróne* with a sort of shy eagerness in her manner.

'There you are, *carina*,' he said, and glanced at

Carol. 'This is my daughter Flavia, who will amuse the boy while we discuss your visit to us – your most unexpected visit. Flavia, take the boy to the orchard and pick yourselves some peaches – ripe ones, *carina*. Eat them in the *grotto* where it is cool and he can see the fish in the pond there.'

'Yes, Papa.' The girl smiled and held out her hand to Teri, but he hesitated and looked up at Carol. She was hesitant herself about letting him go, but the *baróne*'s young daughter seemed nice enough, and she was certainly very pretty with her flyaway eyebrows, her cheekbones high and tapering to a triangular jaw. She had a wide expressive mouth, and eyes of a clear brown.

'The child will be quite safe with Flavia.' Now he spoke with a touch of the whip in his voice. 'Is he one of those pretty boys who clings to his mother all the time?'

'No, he isn't,' she said, stung by his tone of voice. 'Teri isn't a nervous child at all, but this is a strange house to him, and a strange country. *Caro*,' she bent down to him and straightened the collar of his shirt, 'go with the pretty girl and see the fish in the flower house. I – I have to talk with this gentleman and it will be much more fun for you to pick fruit with Flavia.'

'All right, Cally,' he said, and leaning his cheek to hers he whispered: 'She's prettier than her papa, isn't she?'

'Run along with you, Buster.' Carol bit her lip and hoped to heaven the *baróne* had not caught Teri's whispered comment, but children were unconsciously cruel and he was probably used to it. 'And don't eat too many peaches or you'll have the tummyache.'

'Our peaches are sweet, *signora,* at least,' drawled a deep voice above her head, and she dared not look into those sardonic eyes until the door had closed behind his daughter and her son . . . of her heart if not her body.

'Please be seated.' A lean hand gestured at a high-backed chair near his desk and Carol was rather glad to accept his invitation, for now a kind of reaction to the man was setting in and her legs felt curiously shaky. In the first place she hadn't known that Vincenzo had a brother, least of all one whose air of command was impressive and alarming. He was like a dark-browed portrait by Diaz, but one which had gone through flames and emerged as a sort of ruined masterpiece.

He resumed his own high-backed chair and sat there studying her from behind a screen of cigar smoke. Because his scrutiny was so disturbing in that face that still bore traces of Vincenzo, Carol let her gaze fall to the bronze faun which stood on his desk; its workmanship was faultless and its surface seemed to gleam like a real skin. A man of impeccable taste, she told herself. A man who surrounded himself in his private sanctum with objects that had no flaw .. a compensation, perhaps, for the fact that he was himself so marked that many people would instinctively turn away their eyes from his face.

But it wasn't his scars that made her so reluctant to look at him, it was his eyes, steady as a falcon's fixed upon a victim, making her as tense as any hare about to be swooped upon, her skin as tight and cold as if about to be clawed.

As the silence grew she longed for it to be broken,

and her fingers clenched each other when he moved his hand to tip ash into a bronze tray. 'You are not, brutally speaking, the type of woman my brother usually went for,' he said. 'He had a liking for the sensual, not the sensitive ... you are an old-fashioned girl, are you not?'

Carol looked at him then, daring those eyes that penetrated her defences like golden knives. 'What makes you say that, *signore baróne*?'

His eyes dwelt on her hair, braided at the crown of her head so that her neck had a vulnerable look in the white collar of her sedate grey dress.

'Need I elaborate, *signora*?' He gave her that title of a married woman, even though they both knew it to be false on account of that Italian girl with the passionate mouth, who had assured Carol that the *baróne* would kill her for coming here and re-opening old wounds.

'Appearances can be deceptive,' she rejoined. 'You shouldn't be so certain of your own judgments.'

'Ah, but in this instance I am fairly sure. Your hair — can you sit on it when you release it from the plaits?'

'Just about.' A warmth stole into her skin and Carol realised that she was blushing ... it struck her as incredibly erotic to be talking of her hair and its length to this man ... hair that was only let down in the privacy of her bedroom. Was he of the same disposition as Vincenzo? Did his wife have to endure his partiality for other women?

'Most unusual in this day and age.' His eyes held a certain curiosity as they ran over her hair, his black lashes half shading their golden irises. 'Young women with modern ideas of liberation would regard such long hair as a burden. Can you truly sit on it?'

'I've just told you I can, *signore*.'

'And what if I choose to disbelieve you?'

'I would then assume that you consider me a liar.'

'Are you a liar? You arrive here out of the blue, holding a child by the hand, and you tell me that my brother married you.'

'I have my so-called marriage lines, *signore*, if you care to examine them.'

'Why, I wonder, did he marry *you*? Or, at least, go through a form of marriage with you?'

'Oh, he told me why.' Carol tilted her chin and remembered that bitter row with Vincenzo. 'He said I was the type who had to have a wedding ring *before* the wedding night.'

'Ah yes, they would be his sort of words. And so from this *corte e amore* there came a son?'

'Yes, Vincenzo's son.' Her heart twisted, for this man had asked if she was a liar, and what could be a greater lie than for her to pretend that her union with Vincenzo had been real and she had borne the little boy whom she had carried into church and had christened with the Roman name of Terence.

'There is no need to assure me that the boy is a Falcone.' That twist of a smile came and went on the scarred lips. 'My brother lives again in that small piece of humanity—'

'I pray that he won't have his father's ways,' she broke in. 'I hope that all Teri has inherited of Vincenzo is that look of good breeding.'

35

'And for the rest, *signora,* he must take after you, his mother?' The falcon eyes raked her face. 'Are you such an angelic creature, then, with no faults to pass on to your son? Have you no pride, no temper, no dark and secret desires that trouble your sleep at night? Do you never lose patience with other people, and are you always scrupulously honest?'

'I – I try to be as honest as possible.' Her heart thudded and she sensed that this man who had known Vincenzo so well had doubts about her, and he meant to pursue them in his own devious way. 'I'm no angel – I would never pretend to be. White lies are sometimes necessary in order to protect someone who matters.'

'What about black lies, madam?' Now his eyes had a merciless look in them and Carol knew for certain that he was grilling her, and with a certain finesse, leading up to it with a dark velvet interest in her long blonde hair. 'Have you never resorted to one of those?'

'Not about my hair.' She forced a note of flippancy into her voice, needing desperately to divert him from his pursuance of that doubt in his Italian mind that she had ever been one of his brother's women. 'It's my one vanity, or so I like to believe. If I let down my braids will you be convinced of my – veracity?'

'Any man convinced of a woman's veracity is either a dolt or a saint, and I am neither. I have also learned that a woman does no man a favour without exacting something in return. What do you want of me, *English Miss?*'

She almost gasped aloud, for her heart seemed to

leap right into her throat at the way he spoke those last two words, his voice sinking down into a sort of darkness.

'I – I want a better life for Teri than I can give him – that's all, *signore baróne*.' There was a throb in her voice . . . almost a sob.

'That is all?' Smoke curled about his features, losing itself in the thrusting bones and hollows and fearful scars. 'Surely not all – from his mother who gave him life?'

'All right!' She sat there very straight in the high Italian chair and she looked directly into those searching eyes. 'I want to stay with Teri if you say he can live here at Falconetti. But I don't want your charity – I've never taken that from anyone and I've always worked for my bed and board.'

'And what would you like to work at in my house?'

'I – I can help around the *palazzo*, which is obviously a large establishment. I'm unafraid of hard work, *signore*.'

'I have housemaids and a cook, and they would be highly indignant if I took on English help in my very Italian household.'

'I see.' Carol's hands were trembling in her lap, for it had cost her a lot of pride to appeal to this man in this way. 'You will accept Teri, but not me?'

'Have I said so?'

'Not in so many words, but it's there in your face – what you feel.'

'Really, madam? I can hardly feel anything with one side of my face, for the nerves are dead. Perhaps

37

you assume that my heart is dead to go with my face?'

'N-nothing of the sort, *signore*. It just seems obvious to me that I wouldn't fit into your household, and I can almost read your mind as you look at me and see the – the woman Vincenzo lived with in England.'

'Never presume to know my mind.' He spoke curtly and ground out the remains of his cigar in the bronze ashtray. 'It just wouldn't suit me to have my nephew's mother working as a servant in my house.'

'I wouldn't mind—'

'I would, and so it is out of the question.'

'I see.' Hope began to die coldly inside her at the implacability of the *baróne*'s face and voice. 'Hasn't a *palazzo* as large as this one a library of many books? It was my work, caring for books, before – oh, before I worked for my aunts in their tea-room. I love working among books—'

'Truly an old-fashioned girl, eh?'

'Yes – I suppose so.'

'With hair to the base of your spine, or so you claim.'

'Beyond my spine, and I can prove it.'

'Very well!' Something came into his eyes that made her think vividly of Vincenzo; a devil light that cast out responsible thinking and took in its place a moment of sheer recklessness. 'If you can really prove to me that you can sit on your hair, then the job in my library is yours. But if you've been bragging—'

'I never brag, *signore*.' Carol stood up and thrusting from her that first prudish impulse to make a dash from this man who might be far more dangerous than Vincenzo had ever been, she lifted her hands and began

38

the ritual of letting down her light golden hair; a ritual seen only by one other male, and he a small boy of five.

Now in front of a man almost a stranger she released the gleaming serpent of hair until it rolled slowly down her back, uncoiled and alive with motes of gold, dropping down the slimness of her body until it reached past her hips and then her slenderly curved bottom.

She stood there in a stream of sunlight through the high Italian windows and felt curiously naked as the eyes of Rudolph Falcone ran down her body and her unbound hair.

'Sit down,' he ordered.

She did so and the soft tails of her hair were under the curve of her body in the dark chair carved all over with garlands and tiny masks. She could feel herself trembling as the *baróne* rose to his feet and came right round the desk to look at her. He was exceptionally tall, lean as steel sheathed in a suit of dark grey.

'So you win your bet,' he said, and his voice was even darker toned, strewn with gravel that seemed to rake across her skin. 'Stand up again, if you please.'

Again she obeyed him in utter silence and he stepped nearer to her and her breath almost stopped in her throat as he extended one of his darkly beautiful hands and ran his fingers down the soft living gold of her beautiful hair.

'Never cut it,' he said. 'It would be like the destruction of a Verzelini goblet, with coiled serpent tails supporting the delicate bowl. A living serpent of gold, eh?' And suddenly he wrapped the blonde hair right around her body and used it to pull her against him.

39

He held her like that and made her suffer the close impact of his eyes and his face. 'Vincenzo's woman, eh? Why, I wonder, do you tremble?'

'Because you're a stranger to me ...' Carol could feel her heart pressed to him and never had its apprehension been so acute. 'Because you've made me let down my pride in order to beg something of you, and I – I swore that I wouldn't beg anything.'

'A woman will do many things for her child.' His eyes moved searchingly over her face. 'Love is like the *quemedero*, eh? A flame that burns deeply – my face shocks you, does it not?'

'Shocks me, yes.'

'Does it also repel you?'

'No—'

'No?' he mocked. 'One of your white lies, I think, in order not to hurt my feelings. I am beyond being hurt – least of all by Vincenzo's woman.'

A woman! His wife, who might at any moment enter this room and find them like this. 'Please, I'd like to tidy my hair, *signore*.'

'And I,' he said, his voice deep in his throat, 'would like to tangle it.'

'Please – I didn't come here for this.' Suddenly it struck her that he must inevitably think of her as his brother's 'woman' and all that the word implied. Vincenzo had left behind at Falconetti a legal wife, and now she came to the *isola* with a child, and by asking to stay here with that child she laid herself wide open to the inference that she was willing to repay the *baróne* in this way. Her skin felt as if it were scorching and she gave a sudden jerk away from him that tugged at the roots of her hair.

'What do you take me for?' she gasped. 'Let me go before we're seen like this – I don't want to make an enemy of your daughter, or your wife.'

'My wife?' His eyes were suddenly topaz-hard in his dark face. 'Are you pretending that you know nothing at all of Vincenzo's family? You lived with him, yet you profess total innocence of his background!'

'He never talked about his family, so I assumed there had been some kind of – break-up. I certainly never knew that he already had a wife.' She looked up into Rudolph Falcone's eyes and dared him to call her a liar. 'Do you imagine I'd have lived with a man who was married?'

'One way or another you did exactly that, madam.' His eyes were sardonic as they locked with hers. 'You have the evidence in the shape of the boy, have you not? Just how old is he?'

'Five,' she said, and felt a growing antagonism for this man who had a far more subtle and dangerous approach to a woman than the charm used by Vincenzo. He was shrewd and tortured, and like the falcon he wouldn't let go of his prey until he drew blood.

'Why did you wait all this time to come to Falconetti?' he asked. 'Vincenzo has been dead about that length of time, so I assume the child was a mere baby at the time of the accident.'

'Teri was born two months after Vincenzo died,' she said, and she couldn't keep her voice from quaking.

41

Now she was on quicksands, and she could have sunk into them and been glad to be free of this man's eyes and the way they stabbed into her. 'I've tried to give him the things he should have, but I just don't earn enough money. I have my pride, *signore*. I didn't want to turn to Vincenzo's family for help, but Teri is a bright child and I – I want him to have a proper life and not a deprived one.'

'Most commendable, but if Vincenzo never talked of his family then how could you be sure that we could be of assistance to you? We might have been poor people, just able to support ourselves, let alone the child and woman of Vincenzo.'

'For heaven's sake don't keep calling me his *woman*!' A tremor of distress ran all through Carol. 'I believed him to be my husband, and that's no lie. I guessed that his people were well-to-do.'

'Did you love him?' Inexorably came the question. 'In my experience my handsome brother was incapable of being faithful to any woman, and I have the curious feeling that you were never quite his – type.'

'He's dead,' she said quietly. 'The memories are buried with him, and I only care about the boy. Will your wife accept us, *signore*?'

'I doubt it,' he said drily.

'Then—?' Carol looked at him with perplexed eyes.

'I don't happen to be married. Flavia is my foster-child. Her father was my business partner and I became responsible for her when her parents lost their lives in a boating accident along with their young son. Flavia was away at school at the time. Wife! What

42

woman could love *this*?' With an abrupt movement he forced Carol's hand up against his scarred cheek and she couldn't stop herself from crying out. 'It isn't a very romantic face for a woman to touch and kiss, is it?' A cruel mockery lurked in his eyes. 'What woman could caress my face with loving hands?

Equally abruptly he let go of Carol, pulling his fingers free of her long hair. 'I have no wife and it's just as well. The falconmen don't make the best of husbands, and when I had my – accident, I was fortunate not to be blinded. To be blind would be far more insupportable than to be scarred. I, at least, can live with it.'

As he spoke he turned from her so that only the unflawed side of his face was showing; proudly chiselled with high bones that thrust with a kind of hunger against the dark skin. He fingered the bronze faun that stood on his desk and his hands were exactly the same colour and equally well made. 'Stay at Falconetti with your son – and now I had better know your name.'

'It's Carol—' She hastily bit her lip, remembering in time that she no longer had the right to Vincenzo's surname. 'Carol Adams.'

'We had better refer to you as Mrs. Adams for the sake of propriety, for island people can be rather insular in their moral attitudes.' He faced her again and watched with no movement in his eyes the deft way she rearranged her hair, braiding it swiftly and smoothly to the crown of her head.

'Your composure is truly amazing, Mrs. Adams, in the circumstances.'

'I – I was warned that you would probably kill me, *signore*, for daring to come here.'

'Then you have got off lightly, have you not? You will take a glass of wine?'

At her nod he went to a cabinet overlaid by tortoiseshell and took from it a cut-glass decanter and a pair of wine cups. Carol, in need of some ease for her shaken nerves, looked around the room and saw its striking beauty in more detail. The dark mahogany panelling that gleamed like polished armour, and the frescoed ceiling with its rich colours, flying clouds and cloaks, curving limbs and flashing eyes.

'Your wine, Mrs. Adams.' He was standing in front of her, holding towards her the lovely old wine cup encircled by a fresco of tiny imps. As she took it and looked at it with evident pleasure, that faint twist of a smile touched his lips.

'Never drink good wine out of anything but the best containers. Wine, like love, isn't worth the tasting unless it goes to the head and the heart. *Salúte*!'

'*Salúte*,' she echoed, and found the wine superb and certainly potent. 'You have a beautiful house, *signore*. I couldn't believe it when the railway porter called it a *palazzo*.'

'Are you enquiring if we are very rich?' he asked, and with a gesture he invited her to sit down in a deep armchair of red leather. When she sat down he took the companion chair.

'You're bound to think me mercenary, *signore*, but I really mean what I said about working for my keep. I wouldn't want it any other way, and I don't expect

44

Teri to have any legal claims on – on your money.'

'Quite so, he has none! It would have been awkward for you, would it not, if your son had looked like you instead of resembling my brother so unmistakably. I might well have run you off the island had you come here with a blond boy, his eyes the colour of the moonstone.'

Carol looked sharply at the *baróne* when he said that. He was an acutely disturbing man . . . everything about him, his voice, his remarks, his flawed looks that must have been those of a Roman charioteer, a man to whom women would have flown like falcons at a snap of his fingers. Now he had a frightening quality, as if he might enjoy being cruel to a woman, especially if she claimed to care for him.

'You will be kind to Teri?' she asked tensely.

'Oh yes, madam.' He twirled the wine in his frescoed cup. 'I reserve my cruelty for women, and you know it, don't you?'

Carol looked at him and thought to herself that he was *diàvolo* in a way Vincenzo had not been. With his brother it had been a pursuit of pleasure, but with Rudolph it was a kind of sardonic enjoyment in getting into the minds of people and finding out just how vulnerable they might be.

'Yes, I think you could be cruel,' she said.

'And you probably understand why.' His gaze slid across her face. 'This situation is certainly *intrigànte*.'

'Oh, most intriguing,' she said wryly. 'I have placed myself at your uncertain mercy – it seems to have become a habit with me.'

'A habit?' He lifted a black eyebrow. 'You fell a victim to my brother's charm, and now his child has drawn you here despite your misgivings, eh? You are a martyr to your own heart, Mrs. Adams.'

'If you like to put it that way, *messère*.' That Italian word for master slipped out almost unaware, and yet directly she spoke it Carol was aware that it fitted him. He was a masterful man, and he was most certainly the master of all this – a superb *palazzo* on an island, who had made her do something she had never done for Vincenzo ... she had let down her hair for Rudolph Falcone in order to stay here with the child who was not hers.

Her fingers tightened on her wine cup ... he must never learn the real truth, for he wasn't the type to forgive anyone for cheating him in a game of chance.

'You are sitting there forming an opinion of me,' he said. 'May I know it, for it amuses me to collect the impressions of women regarding the man I am behind this awful face.'

Carol flinched at his words ... yes, it must be awful for a man who had once been as handsome as one of the gods to look in a woman's eyes and see there her instinctive recoil from his burns. Pity he would dread and scorn, and so Carol resorted to the truth that lay in her mind regarding him. 'Yes, I'll tell you my impression of you, *messère*. You are like one of those Roman governors of long ago, who sat in the best seats at the Circus Maximus to watch the Christians being fed to the lions.'

'A charming image, madam.'

'Is it altogether a distorted image?' she asked.

'No.' He shook his head. 'The ancestory of the Falcones goes far back into Roman times and my genes are undoubtedly shaded by the pagan past – and what of you, eh? In far-off days were you a Christian slave with only your remarkable hair to cover your white body?'

His voice and accent, his very way of looking at her created a vivid mental image of a ruthless centurion with his eyes fixed upon a Christian girl offered up to the wicked delight of the Roman crowd, their jeers and laughter echoing around the arena as she suffered just to provide sport for them.

Had she been invited to stay at the *palazzo* just to provide sport for this man, who could never have been gentle even before the accident to his face had seared the memory of pain deep into his flesh and bones?

'Yes,' he murmured, reading her thoughts in her eyes. 'Every man must have his *divertiménto*, and the modern circus is all nets and teddy bears. It's a small return for what I shall do for your son, born as he was on the wrong side of the blanket.'

Carol flushed and hated him for that . . . only her love for Teri kept her in this room with this man. In order to get for the boy the things to which his birth entitled him she had to put up with the *baróne*'s tormenting remarks; she had to bite on the bullet and not give way to the urge to tell him to go to the devil. He knew she was fighting with her temper, it was there in his eyes. Very softly he laughed at her, daring her to refuse his patronage for the boy.

'You don't like me, do you, Mrs. Adams?' he

47

mocked. 'Unlike Vincenzo I can't be charmed by wide grey eyes and a long creamy neck carrying a weight of blonde hair. I'm iron, madam, where he was smouldering blood and nerves for anything in skirts. There is probably more of Vincenzo in the boy than there is of you, and you did right to bring him here, even if it did take you five years. Stay! It's a settled thing!'

'Do I kiss your hand for being so generous?' she couldn't resist asking. 'I suppose as master of all this you can't help your arrogance.'

'I don't doubt that I'd be arrogant if I had only a lemon cart to trundle around the streets,' he said. 'We are human beings, madam, not dolls. We are flawed by our kind of manufacture as a Lenci doll could never be.'

'It – it does occur to me, *signore baróne,* that you could provide an income for Teri – the one that Vincenzo had, perhaps? Then we shouldn't have to impose on your hospitality and I could take a flat in Rome and find work there—'

'Be quiet!' he ordered, and stood up so he towered over the chair in which Carol sat. 'The boy is part of this family and he belongs here, and as he's still quite young he should have his mother with him. You may not like the idea of living under my jurisdiction, but it's what you came for and it's what you have. What did you think? That the child had a white-haired grandfather who would dote on the pair of you?'

'Perhaps.' She leapt to her feet, but he was still a good deal taller, making her feel that he always had the advantage by reason of his height and the terror of his face. Her heart felt gripped, shaken, when he looked

48

directly down at her and she had to endure the devastation of a face that must have been so striking. 'I suppose in my heart I did hope that Vincenzo had parents who would understand my plight.'

'Your plight, madam, is that you leapt into Vincenzo's arms without thinking. You must have been a mere girl – eighteen, I would say. The wife he left behind him was about the same age. Our mother was alive then, and it was she who arranged the marriage. I said at the time that it was a mistake to force the girl upon him, but he made such a bad reputation for himself among the kind of girls that our mother couldn't accept into the family that she hoped to subdue him by making a family man of him. It didn't work, eh? He ran off and collected another bride for himself . . . I think it a good thing that my mother is not alive. She wouldn't have understood your plight, Mrs. Adams. She would have had you thrown out of Falconetti, along with the boy. Her pride could not have stood for a grandson born illegitimately.'

Carol shivered at the word. This was her darling Teri whom they discussed in this cold and cynical way. Oh, how could she hope that he and she would be happy in this palace of a house, ruled over by a man of arrogant hardness?

She didn't doubt that he had a sensuous love of the beautiful things he had collected around him; his fingers played over them as if they produced a soundless music for him alone. But she had the sure feeling that few people had touched his heart . . . least of all a strange woman who came here assuming the motherhood of Vincenzo's child; the dead brother who in his life had deserted a young and legal wife and probably broken his mother's heart by his desertion.

Vincenzo had worshipped 'love's warm sweet mouth,' but Rudolph had said he was made of iron, and Carol believed him.

Whatever had happened to his face enclosed him in armour that would have few inlets to his hardened heart, and she was about to place Teri and herself in his hands.

She looked at him and felt as if her heart were trembling, and never before had she been so aware of the fateful strangeness of life . . . as if one stood in the wings of a great theatre and waited for a curtain to rise on scenes that would terrify, perhaps thrill, and cause pain.

Her heart raced . . . this moment was like a casket that opened slowly . . . slowly.

'Finish your wine,' he said, and she glanced dazedly at the garnet-red wine in the lovely old cup and lifted it slowly to her lips. It ran warm and enlivening down her throat.

'Better?' he drawled. 'You looked for a moment as if you might faint. Have you and the boy had any food?'

'We had breakfast,' she faltered. 'Before we caught the bus to the lake—'

'That was hours ago,' he said curtly. He leaned to his desk and pressed the bell on it. Then he moved to the windows in his iron-grey suit that was so faultlessly tailored, fitting like a second skin to his lean and supple body. From the back he had the *nobilezza* air from his black hair to his handmade shoes. *Il signor baróne*, who gazed from the windows upon his vast property, imperious as a Roman of old.

'Come see the lake as the sun goes down,' he ordered.

Carol walked slowly towards him, feeling the tremor in her legs that was caused as much by this encounter with him as by the need for food. She halted beside his tall figure and looked down upon the Lake of Lina that enclosed this island that seemed so many miles from Chalkleigh and the Copper Jug, where the gossip would be rife that Carol had followed her sister Cynara's example and run off to foreign parts ... no doubt at the beckoning of a man.

A nervous little smile tugged at Carol's lips. Could the Aunts but see her, alone in the flaming gold of an Italian sunset with a man whose hair and sideburns were like the cheek-flanges of a Roman helmet, and whose eyes as they briefly flicked her face were like those of a falcon.

She stared at the lake that was shot with red and gold in the glow of the falling sun, just as if gems had been spilled on the water. The water reeds stood dark in that drifting light, bristling and bending in the coming breeze. The air drifting through the windows had a coolness to it and the tang of lemons.

The incandescence of the sunset was a beauty bordering on fear. It was of heaven, the realm of love and death.

The little pools of shadow seemed to hold menace at the lakeside; everything brooded, the house, the master, and the distant mountains. The golden shadows deepened and crept over the gardens of broken statuary and stone paths leading to hidden places. The sky overhead was a wonderful cloak of a thousand mixed colours, and a great cloud of mauve vines whispered and moved on the wall beneath the windows.

'No artist could ever reproduce that in all its living beauty, not even the old masters.' That deep voice of the *baróne*'s seemed to play over Carol's nerve-ends. 'We have paintings and tapestries in the *galleria* that are superb, but each evening I prefer to stand here and watch nature at work with her superior talents. Have you ever seen a sunset like that one, Mrs. Adams?'

'Never so vivid, *messère*. It was almost – frightening.'

'Great beauty is somehow like that,' he agreed. 'We stand in awe of it, fascinated, and yet if we could touch it, we would choose not to.'

As he spoke Carol looked up at the hard Latin sculpture of his unmarked profile; there had been a strange and brooding note in his voice, as if he might have known such beauty in a living person . . . a beauty not to be touched by a man.

A silence hung between them, and it was broken as the door of the panelled room was opened to admit the tall, slender figure of a woman. 'You rang, Rudi?' She had a rather charming voice, but what struck Carol was that anyone should dare to address the *baróne* in such a fashion.

'Ah, it's you, Gena.' He moved from the shadows and at his desk he turned on a lamp so that Carol had a better impression of the young woman. She had striking features, with eyes of dark topaz which at the moment held a sparkle of curiosity.

'Bedelia informed me that we had a visitor – she was in a bit of a state, Rudi, and said something about a woman coming here with a boy who is being palmed off on us as a nephew. It's all very intriguing, but is it true?'

'The boy is Vincenzo's,' said the *baróne*, without any hesitation. 'You will be in no doubt when you see him. This young woman, Gena, was another of his – victims.'

'Oh – I see.' The topaz eyes swept up and down Carol's slim figure in the grey and white dress, coming to rest on her rather pale face under the crown of blonde hair.

'Mrs. Adams, meet my sister Angelina, whom we call Gena.'

'How do you do?' Carol managed a troubled smile. 'My first name is Carol – I prefer to be called that, for it seems that I'm not a married woman after all.'

'Really? Vince was a deceiver ever!' Gena smiled, and her handsome face softened considerably. 'They call me Gena because I'm no angel – there never was a Falcone who aspired to heavenly heights. Are you going to stay with us?'

'The *baróne* has been good enough to say that we might, *signora*.'

'It's *signorina*.' Gena waved a ringless hand. 'No man would dare to take on a female Falcone, for we're far too arrogant and fond of our own way. Where is

53

this boy who has sent Bedelia into hysterics?'

'He's with Flavia,' said the *baróne*. 'This young woman needs a meal, Gena, and an apartment. Will you arrange those for me? The boy will wish to be close to his mother, for he's only five years old. He's a Falcone right enough and his place is with us.'

'If you say so, Rudi.' His sister spoke with a kind of casual indifference, as if she left all important decisions to her brother and didn't question his authority. 'You do realize, *mio*, that Bedelia isn't going to be happy to have here the son and heir she wanted for Vince, but that is your problem.'

'Most things are,' he said drily. 'The child is five, there is no doubt about his relationship to us, and whatever our faults, Gena, we don't shirk our responsibilities, eh? Bedelia will have to accept my decision to let Mrs. Adams and her son live here at Falconetti.'

'Then come with me,' Gena said to Carol. 'Did you bring any luggage with you?'

'Yes. Oh, it wasn't that I was all that certain we'd be welcome here, but I – I had no real intention of returning home. Teri and I would have found a room for ourselves in Rome and I'd have got a job there.'

Carol turned impulsively to the *baróne*. 'I want to thank you again, *signore*, for making Teri welcome and giving me that job.'

'What job?' Gena asked, quirking a slim brow in a way that made her look like her brother. 'Rudi, you aren't going to make this poor girl work for her keep?'

'It was her idea.' His eyes dwelt sardonically on

54

Carol's face. 'She assumed, correctly, that we have here a large library and she has been trained in the art of caring for books. I have said that she may work in the library and repair any volumes that need attention. I have noticed myself that endpapers and covers are loose on a number of the books and it seems a pity to let them worsen when we have with us a willing pair of hands. The library is at your disposal, Mrs. Adams, but the child comes first and I know that you would prefer to have him in your charge. Does he yet go to school?'

'He had just started school – is there one on the *isola*, *signore*? He speaks excellent Italian and he's very bright—'

'Of course he is.' The *baróne* accepted that as if it were a foregone conclusion that any member of his family would be intelligent, at least. 'There is a school, but I think it might be better if I arranged a tutor for him.'

'Oh, just because he's a Falcone?' Carol exclaimed. 'I want him to have friends—'

'He will find his friends on the estate among the children of my staff, but the reason I suggest a tutor is that we are quite a financially secure family.' His eyes fixed Carol, hard and cold as stones in his scarred face. 'Would you want anything to happen to your son? I have enemies, and I have money, and kidnapping is not so rare in Italy as it might be in England. Do I make myself clear?'

He not only made himself clear, but his face and his eyes frightened Carol as never before.

'Yes, *signore*.' Her voice shook and when she placed

55

the wine cup on his desk it almost toppled off and sent her heart into her throat. She almost felt like dashing off in search of Teri and taking him away from the dangers and tensions of this house, and she gave a visible shudder when Rudolph Falcone reached out and took her by the wrist. His fingers were dark and lean against her skin, and their touch was warm and curiously penetrating.

'Every Eden has its serpent, Mrs. Adams, and Falconetti is no exception. There are no dream islands where the sun always shines and the shadows never fall, if that is what you hoped to find.'

'I – I don't know what I hoped for – the best I could find for Teri, perhaps, but I don't want him hurt!'

She stared up at the *baróne*'s face in the lamplight, dark and made sinister by his scars.

A quiver ran across her own face and she wished desperately that he would remove his hand from her arm … but instead his fingers tightened as the door burst open and Teri came dashing in, flying headlong towards her with fruit juice and laughter all over his face that was a small replica of Vincenzo's.

'Cally, it's smashing here!' He paused breathless in front of her. 'They have horses and ponies, and I've had three peaches and sat on the swing in the orchard. Let's live here for always, Cally! It's a palace, you know, and – and—'

He broke off and stared at the *baróne*, and the way he was gripping Carol's wrist.

'Don't do that,' he muttered.

'Do what, young man?'

'Don't touch my mummy.'

There was an instant of acute silence, and then Gena broke it by laughing. 'Jealous little devil, aren't you? Come here and let me look at you.'

Gena took hold of him and swung him to face her; she gazed down at his grubby, pouting face, and a half-sad look came into her topaz eyes. 'You are the image of your papa, aren't you, little boy? But I wonder if you're going to take after him – he was acquisitive but not really possessive.' Gena flung a look at Rudolph. 'There might be a dash of you in this child, Rudi. Are you amused?'

'Profoundly,' he drawled. 'Your release, madame,' he added, letting go of Carol. 'It would seem that your son wishes to stay with us, would you not agree?'

'Yes,' she sighed, and looking at Teri she saw the Falcone heritage in his face . . . passionate, self-willed, in the frame where it belonged.

Falconetti!

CHAPTER THREE

THE ceiling had a great moulded scene of Apollo chasing Daphne in and out of the laurel trees. Serpents entwined on the tall bedposts, and curtains, draperies and upholstery were all hand-woven.

A pair of rooms, interjoined by a white stone archway, with enormous closets embellished with brass and mother-of-pearl, and on the dressing-table in Carol's room an assortment of Italian flowered pots and bowls reflected in a mirror huge as a Roman shield.

Teri was entranced by the half-moon of steps that led up to Carol's huge bed, and amused himself hopping up and down them, and tracing with his sticky fingers the carvings on the bedposts. 'Snakes and acorns,' he murmured, 'toolips and toadstools.'

Gena grinned at Carol and leaned back in the cane-seated rocking chair with a cheroot in her hand. 'Mustn't it be great to be a carefree child? We don't realize the perfection of it until we're too old to start again. Would you like to start all over and have things less complicated for you?'

'Who wouldn't?' Carol pressed a table napkin to her lips and felt very much refreshed by a delicious cup of coffee and several sandwiches of tender and tasty ham. 'I expect for most people there's a point in their lives when they wish they could turn back the pages and start anew, aware of their mistakes and prepared to avoid them.'

'I gather,' Gena leaned forward and lowered her voice, 'that you'd avoid my brother if you could erase the last half dozen years from your life.'

'Yes—' And then Carol glanced at Teri, who had curled up in the centre of the bed and lay there with the wooden redskin they had unpacked from his suitcase. 'But then I wouldn't have my boy – I'd have nothing.'

'That's just it, isn't it?' Gena smiled ironically. 'Each cloud has its silver lining, and I don't care if it is a cliché. I guess if we regret our mistakes and wish them wiped out, we lose out on the bits and pieces of joy we collect along the way. By the way, if my speech strikes you as being rather Americanized it's because I lived in New York for several years and sang at the Metropolitan Opera House. Only in the chorus, but it was enormous fun, and then Rudi had his – accident, and I came home to Italy to keep him company and to keep house for him.'

Directly Gena spoke of her brother's accident with that angry hint of hesitation before the word, Carol wanted to ask about it. Gena tossed ash from her cheroot and her face held a brooding expression.

'Don't get me wrong,' she said, 'I don't begrudge being here, for it wasn't as if my voice was ever good enough to land me lead singing roles – nice enough, but I can't hit those real high notes. No, I had good times and I'm quite content to live here. It's just that Rudi will never marry, and when I remember how attractive he was – my dear, he could have had any woman he

59

fancied. He adopted Flavia, and though she's a dear child she wants to return to her convent school to become a member of their Order. Rudi will give his permission, of course, if it's what she truly wants. *Dio mio*, to be a nun! It wouldn't suit me.'

Gena gave her warm chuckle and crossed her long slim legs. 'Yes, I had a great time in America. I've had lovers, Carol. Does that confession shock you?'

'I'm surely the last person to be shocked.' Carol smiled slightly and was unsurprised that a woman like Gena, with her humorous eyes and her generous mouth, should have enjoyed the company of men. It only surprised Carol that she was unmarried ... was her loyalty to her brother too strong to allow of it?

'Because of Vince?' Gena narrowed her eyes through her cheroot smoke as she gazed at Carol. 'Because you had his child?'

'Yes—' The great lie had to be a convincing one and having committed herself to it Carol was prepared to act the part for all that Teri was worth. She didn't enjoy deceiving people, but she didn't think the *baróne*'s reaction would be a very gentle one if he found out that she hadn't even lived with Vincenzo, let alone borne him that small handsome edition of a Falcone. She strongly suspected that she would be shown the door and told to make herself scarce, and it wouldn't worry that man if Teri screamed for her. She had the feeling that he was hardened to the pain of other people.

'Vince was ever an unholy terror,' Gena admitted. 'We Falcones are a rather headstrong lot. Tell me, what is it like being the mother of a boy and having no man to share his growing up?'

'Worrying more than anything.' Desperately so, Carol could have added, especially when that child was not your own.

'Were you crazy about Vince?' Gena ran her eyes over Carol's face.

'At the beginning – then I thought him my dream suitor, I suppose. I was very young and carried away by his looks.'

'Yes, he was a stunner, and he found out very early that he could make fools of women. Did you know about Bedelia before you came here?'

'Oh no! I shouldn't have come had I known that I wasn't – that he'd married me under false pretences.'

'Why shouldn't you come here? Vince made you a mother, and Rudi has enough money to see that neither of you go without. You should have come before, when Teri was a baby and it must have been difficult for you to manage.'

'Your brother the *baróne* intimated that your mother wouldn't have accepted us.'

'Probably not as residents here, but Rudi would have made sure you were provided with an income.'

'Is he tremendously well off?' Carol nibbled a sweet biscuit and thought of what he had said about the danger of kidnapping.

'As wealth is measured these days, with exorbitant tax on income. He's a designer of high-speed motor engines, both for use on the road and the water. He designed the Spada and it's made a mint. Didn't you know that Vince had this sort of background?'

'He spoke very little about his family and I – I wouldn't probe.' Carol remembered why and couldn't stop the old hurt from coming into her eyes; the disillusion and the disenchantment. 'I guessed from the look of him that he came from a good family—'

'Good!' Gena laughed cynically. 'We've breeding, my dear, but hardly your sort of goodness. Breeding, brains and beauty, the three requisites for being bad and usually getting away with it.'

'I don't think you're bad,' Carol said. 'Cynical, perhaps.'

'And sinful, though I daresay Rudi likes to think that I'm a proper sort of Italian woman, waiting in dewy-eyed expectancy for the right man to come along.' Gena smiled and dropped a sandal from her foot and wriggled her long toes. 'Feet are sensuous things, aren't they? I like a man to stroke mine with the very ends of his fingers – my boy-friends have been Americans, you know, and that would shock Rudi, who is one hundred per cent Latin. God, he was the best looking guy in Italy before that bitch—'

Gena broke off sharply. 'We have an American on the *isola* at the present time. Saul Stern is his name. He's a writer of film and television scripts and he's working on something right now. Rudi rented him a beach house belonging to the estate – he's rather attractive, in that tough New York way that I rather like. Women are funny creatures. We go through our lives always liking the same type of man, and I have this weakness for Yanks. How about you, Carol? Is it always going to be the dark, smouldering Latin type?'

'I hope not!' Carol spoke the words in almost a panic. 'I have no plans to make a fool of myself with any other man. I just want to make a good life for Teri – my happiness will come from that.'

'You hope!' Gena looked sceptical. 'It's okay if a girl is born like Flavia, who wants to give herself to the chaste life, but you've had a lover, Carol, and you've had a baby. You can't suddenly turn off your natural feelings just because you've been hurt by one man. It would be a kind of starvation of your real self.'

'I can stand it,' said Carol, feeling an unbearable fraud at the way she had taken in these people. She had had no lover, and when Teri was born she had sat in a waiting-room while her sister Cynara suffered the birth pangs. Her body felt on fire with guilt and she suddenly stood up and went to the big bed where Teri had fallen sound asleep.

'He's tired out, poor pet,' she murmured. 'We've been travelling for hours and it was rather hot on the bus.'

'My dear, you must be tired yourself.' Gena stubbed her cheroot and slipped her foot into her sandal. 'Have you everything you need? I guess you won't feel like coming down to dinner tonight?'

'Oh no.' Carol had never felt less like facing this family which she had so far succeeded in fooling, and all she wanted right now was to be safely alone with Teri. 'I'll make an early night of it, and please believe that I'm deeply grateful to all of you for making us welcome at Falconetti.'

'Thank Rudi, my dear. He's the *padrone* here and the one who makes the important decisions. It may have helped that you're rather a nice-looking creature, with exceptionally pretty hair—'

'What do you mean?' Carol looked at Gena with a sudden alarm in her eyes. 'Why has it helped that I – I've nice hair?'

'Rudi is a man, *cara*.' Gena looked amused by Carol's alarm. 'Very much so, unless you didn't notice and were concentrating only upon his scars? They're frightening, I know, but his eyes are still as keen as they always were and I'm willing to bet that he noticed your hair and your fair skin that takes a blush so attractively – oh, don't let it panic you. My brother knows the effect that his face has on women and he'd never risk being hurt by one of them – never again!'

'Again?' Carol could feel the sudden tension in the room, as if a coldness had crept in, and a sense of those dark passions that could exist between a man and woman. 'Was it—?'

'Yes.' Gena's face was suddenly as hard as if carved in marble. 'The slim and delicate hand of a woman did it – with vitriol. He was lucky not to lose his sight.'

'How absolutely awful!' Carol had gone so white that her eyes looked intensely violet. 'But why? I – I thought perhaps there had been a fire and he'd been hurt in it.'

'One of those emotional fires, Carol, in which a man and a woman are sometimes caught. An inferno almost as terrible as the real thing.'

'But why – how could anyone do such a thing?' Carol

shuddered as she thought of it, the burning acid, searing into his face, creating an agony which he would never be able to forget. It was far more terrible than being trapped in a fire, for that was a natural sort of hazard, but to have acid thrown at you – instinctively Carol threw her hands up against her own face in a self-protective attitude. Her imagination was vivid and she had a fearful mental picture of those fine Italian features being destroyed while a woman looked on, the empty vitriol bottle in her slim, cruel hand. What could have made her so bitter, so revengeful that she put her mark on a man with corrosive acid?

'You ask why.' Gena shrugged her shoulders. 'I have asked Rudi that question and he has never answered it, and when my brother puts up a shield of reserve then it's useless to try and penetrate it. All I can tell you is that the woman fled and my brother never had a warrant taken out against her. It was a love-hate quarrel, that's about all I know. He never talks about it.'

'How could anyone love and hate to that degree?' Carol asked.

'Deep people often do, my dear. Will the little boy want a milky drink before you put him to bed?'

'He likes Horlicks, if that would be all right? Otherwise just warm milk with a teaspoon of sugar.'

'They'll probably have Horlicks in the kitchen. I'll tell one of the maids to bring it up, with a glass of wine for you. I insist. It will help you to sleep, for I've always found that it's never easy to drop off in a strange bed in an unknown house, and this is a very large one – the bed as well, eh?'

Carol glanced at the great bed and nodded. 'You're being very kind to us, *signorina*.'

'Please call me Gena. *Molto bene, questa la vita.*'

'Good night.' Such was life, indeed.

When the door had closed behind Gena, the room seemed larger than ever and Carol gave way to a shudder of sheer nerves and stood there with her arms clasped around her own body. Had she known all this about the Falcones would she have come here like this, imposing on them – in a way? She gazed at the small, still figure of Teri, his redskin on the bed beside him, and she felt the familiar ache of love for him. There had never been any other soul as close to her as the boy was; she couldn't say that she and Cynara had been all that close even though they had been twins. There had been none of that soul communication that people spoke about in connection with sisters born in the same hour, and there had never been all that much alikeness in their ways. Cynara had shown a preference for the male sex at the very start of her teens, but for Carol that awareness had not awoken until the entry of Vincenzo into her life. He had kindled love in her heart, and then had crushed it out so completely that Carol couldn't imagine herself being starry-eyed over a man ever again.

In fact she now felt frightened by the dark sides there were to the emotion called love.

Her fingers crept to her own cheek, smooth and softly hollowed, and she recalled the feel of the *baróne*'s scars when he had forced her hand to his face and made her touch him.

66

A woman had done that to him ... how then could he ever harbour gentle feelings towards any other woman? The searing pain of the acid would have penetrated to his heart and burned out of it all the kinder aspects of love and desire. He might even feel tempted to be cruel to anyone who tried to get close to him, for how could he ever trust again, ever truly believe that his face was lovable?

He had said it, hadn't he? That he reserved his cruelty for women?

At that moment Teri stirred awake and lay looking at her with his great dark eyes.

'What's the matter, Cally?' He struggled into a sitting position and sleepily blinked his long lashes. 'You have ever such a funny look on your face.'

'It's my natural look, Buster.' She sat down on the bed and drew him close to her heart. 'Well, *caro*, it looks as if we're going to live in this island palace. Do you like the idea?'

He nodded against her and clasped his arms about her neck. 'Is that tall man with the terrible face really my uncle, Cally?'

'Yes, and you mustn't think of his face as being terrible. He was in an – accident and he can't help his scars. He's being very kind to us by letting us stay here and you must always be a good boy to him and never, never mention his face. Do you understand?'

'I'm not afraid of him, Cally,' Teri insisted. 'He's nice on one side, isn't he? I'll look at that side and then I won't get shivery in my tummy.'

She smiled and kissed his ruffled hair. 'That's my

Buster! Now how about having a wash before I put you to bed?'

'Can I sleep in here with you, Cally?' His arms clung closer and she felt him glance over to the archway that led into that other large room with the bed that was a lot too big for one small boy. A smaller bed would have to be found for him, and some brighter furnishings, otherwise he would never be persuaded to sleep on his own. The *baróne*, she suspected, had some firm ideas about the upbringing of boys and he'd hardly be pleased if she made a baby of his nephew.

'For tonight, *caro*,' she said. 'Tomorrow we'll make your own room look much nicer and then you won't mind sleeping there like a big boy, now will you?'

'No,' he said hesitantly. 'It's a very big house, isn't it? You should see the stables all full up with horses. Flavia showed me the big black horse that her papa rides, and he tossed his head ever so high and had steam coming out of his nose.'

Um, she thought, he sounds like his master!

'Come along, honey bunch,' she lifted Teri off the bed, 'let's go and clean your face and hands.'

The bathroom was also large, with a deep green-tiled bath tub that fascinated the boy because it was let into the floor and had steps leading down into it, like a mini swimming-pool. Back home at the Copper Jug the bathroom had been a converted back room with a narrow white tub and cold white walls. But here on the walls were mosaics of sea scenes, and Teri re-discovered King Neptune and his court of mermaids and he stood there entranced while Carol ran water into the marble

68

pedestal wash-basin.

'I've never ever seen a bathroom like this one, Cally. It's 'normous and just like a sea cave.'

Carol had never seen one like it herself. 'It's *bella*,' she agreed, and thought to herself that Rudolph Falcone lived here in his island palace like one of the nobles of the Medici times, shut off from the rest of the world where there were too many eyes to stare at his face.

She caught sight of her own face in a large, bold-framed mirror on the wall, and she felt anew that clutch of alarm at what Gena had said about her appearance having softened the hard heart of her brother. She saw her own vulnerable look, the sea-green lighting of the bathroom making her hair and skin seem unreal in their fairness. She had let down her hair for the man, but not to seduce him; not to make him imagine that she was free with her kisses.

'Do you like it here, Cally?' Teri stood there, wriggling a bit when she applied the face flannel.

'It's a beautiful house, Buster, but like you I feel a bit strange in it. I expect in a few days we'll be more used to the atmosphere.'

'Then we're never going home to the Jug?' he asked, and he suddenly gave her the quick, mischievous smile of a small clown. 'I'm glad Auntie Rachel isn't here with us, for she was always scolding me, and she said I ought to be put in a home. What's a home, Cally, and why should I be put in one? Is it like the dogs' home where they take all the strays?'

'You're as full of questions as a pumpkin is of pips!'

Carol smiled as she wiped his face, but inwardly she was fuming. Aunt Rachel had been furious when she had brought Teri home as a tiny baby, for the Aunts had hoped that Cynara, who during the last six months of her pregnancy had lived in rooms in London, would sign away the baby so he was taken for adoption and the dreaded breath of scandal then receded from their door. But in her fashion Cynara had loved Vincenzo and she had begged Carol to live with her in London and between them they would bring up Vincenzo's child. That had been the agreement, and then on the day of Cynara's discharge from the hospital she had vanished, leaving Carol to cope alone with the dark-haired infant who then, and for always, had stormed her heart with his huge eyes and his helplessness.

Carol had found it impossible to part with Teri, and had thought it would be better for both of them if she arranged with her aunts to go on living with them, helping out in the tearoom, in an environment she was accustomed to. Being all alone in London with a small baby had seemed too much of a challenge at the time, but now she had the feeling that she would have coped. At least it would have saved her from the persistent nagging of the Aunts, who lived in constant dread that Cynara would reappear and claim the child, and therefore reveal to their clientele that they had a niece who had *sinned*.

Oh yes, in many ways were the Aunts a pair of Victorians, and Carol could only wonder at herself for enduring the tensions that were never at rest behind the shell-ruched curtains of the Copper Jug.

She had dared to make her escape from all that, but it couldn't be denied that she had fled from petty tyrants only to find herself in the lair of a veritable dragon who carried the scars of his own brush with love and hate.

When she and Teri returned to her bedroom they found that a maid had brought a steaming cup of Horlicks with some chocolate finger biscuits, and a fluted glass of wine for Carol. The various standard lamps set about the big room cast pools of soft light on the floor, islanded with rugs, and on the panels where big-framed paintings hung. Teri hopped up the half-moon of steps and dived into the bed, and there he sat sipping his drink, while Carol unbound her hair and began to brush it.

'It's better than a dog's home,' Teri announced. 'D'you reckon he'll let me ride one of the ponies, Cally?'

'If you ask him very politely,' she said, 'and remember to call him Uncle Rudolph.'

Teri gazed at her big-eyed over the rim of his beaker. 'It's a very long name and that lady with the laughy eyes called him Rudi.'

'That, my Buster, is because she is the *baróne's* sister and entitled to – to an affectionate name for him, just as I have my name for you. To you, *caro*, he is Uncle Rudolph and don't you forget it. He's an important man, remember, and we must show a proper respect for his hospitality.'

'Will we see much of him, Cally?' Teri nibbled a chocolate finger and his own straight dark brows made that single line across his small but decidedly Italian nose as he watched the lamplight shimmering on Carol's hair. 'He touched you!'

'It was nothing.' But even as she spoke Carol could feel the wave of warmth sweeping over her, and that clutch of panic in the pit of her stomach. The *baróne* was absolute master here, and in his eyes she was the woman who had lived with Vincenzo and borne a love child. She had to accept the bitter with the sweet, and there was a certain sweetness in having this apartment to share with Teri, with its great carved door that secured for them the kind of privacy very much denied at the Copper Jug. The amber-shaded lamps gave a light that was softly golden, and though large the apartment was warmed by radiators, for as in most southern countries the nights were cool after the sun died away.

She tucked Teri into her bed and bent to kiss his forehead. 'Sleep well, *caro*, and have good dreams.'

'Goo-night, Cally.' Already his lashes were falling sleepily to cover the big dark eyes. 'It's ever such a soft bed.'

'Yes, isn't it?' She sat there on the bedside watching as he fell asleep, and she assured herself that she didn't care what attitude the *baróne* took towards her. This was where Teri belonged and it had been worthwhile coming here for his sake.

Glass of wine in hand, her long hair falling around her slim body like a pale silk cloak, Carol wandered about the room getting acquainted with its atmosphere.

The massive furniture of dark mahogany had some strange and fascinating carvings worked into it, and the light of the lamps glimmered on the wood and made it gleam. She made out tiny figures grouped as if to dance the *tarantella*, a shepherd carrying a lamb, and fat little *angeli*. Carol stroked her fingers across the patina of the old wood and wondered which projection of carved flower or tiny head opened the inevitable secret passage in this Italian suite.

From all accounts the Latin nobles had loved to build into their houses these concealed openings that made it possible for intrigues to be carried on, and it wouldn't have surprised Carol if such an opening lay behind the panelling of this room.

She stroked the long hand-woven curtains and listened to the ticking of a lovely Venetian clock. The borders of the curtains were richly embroidered, and beyond lay deep window embrasures, quite sheer above the lake.

The Lake of Lina, with its wavelets and overhanging trees; its air of night-time sadness. And out there in the darkness the cicadas made their ceaseless fiddling while the stars burned and the big moths floated by like ghosts.

A perfect setting, Carol thought, for a Byronic master who had been tortured by a former love; a man who sought solitude, his passions and angers kept firmly in hand, cruel or kind as the mood took him.

Carol cradled her wine glass in her fingers and felt the chiselled facets against her skin. She would have been beautiful, that woman who had loved and hated him, and each time he looked into a mirror at his own face he would be unable to forget her. It would have been a love quite terrible to have led to a quarrel so intense, and with a shiver at such consequences Carol turned away from the windows and let the curtains fall back into place, hiding the dark things of the night.

She placed her wine glass on a table and went into the bathroom to take a warm shower, which might help to relax her. She had hung her robe in there in readiness, and after bundling her hair into a shower cap, she stepped under the water and closed her mind to everything but the warm pelt of it. Back home there had never been this kind of luxury and she enjoyed it to the full and it was a good half hour before she was towelled dry and casually enclosed in the folds of her robe. She released her hair and wandered back into her bedroom, only to pause sharply in the archway, a hand flying to her throat.

Silhouetted against the lamplight was the figure of a woman and she was bending over the bed, staring silently at the sleeping figure of Teri.

There was something about her intentness that petrified Carol. She sensed danger to the boy and wanted to leap forward and push that dark-haired, silent figure away from him. But that would be melodramatic, and after her first thrust of surprise she recognized the woman as Bedelia – the young wife from whom Vincenzo had run away, turning up in England to bring emotional havoc into the lives of Carol and her sister Cynara.

'Good evening.' Carol forced herself to speak in a

matter-of-fact voice as she stepped into the room and tightened the sash of her robe. 'You will be careful not to wake him, won't you? He's had a long day and is tired out.'

At the sound of Carol's voice the young woman swung round from the bedside and smouldering in her eyes was her resentment that Carol and the boy had been allowed to remain at the *palazzo*. They stared at each other, two women who had believed in Vincenzo and been bitterly disillusioned.

'You had no right to bring *him* here.' Bedelia gestured at the bed. 'I was Vincenzo's real wife, and that child is a—'

'Don't you dare say it!' Carol spoke in a low, fierce voice. 'Teri is only a child and I won't have him insulted by you, or frightened in any way. If you dare to do so, then I'll go straight to the *baróne* and have you stopped. Believe me, I didn't come here with the idea of – of hurting you, *signora*, for I didn't even know about you. I believed Vincenzo Falcone to be a single man, otherwise I'd never have married him.'

'Why should I believe you?' Bedelia thrust with a ringed hand at her blue-black hair, and stared hatefully at the blonde hair falling so abundantly over the shoulders of Carol's mauve wrapper. 'You are a woman on the make, that is all too evident to me, but you have taken in the *baróne* with your innocent airs, and your son. I suppose you are hoping that he will make the child his heir, as he is never likely to marry himself.'

'Why isn't he likely to marry?' Carol asked. 'He's still

a fairly young man, and he has a large estate to pass on.'

'The woman would have to be blind.' Bedelia flung up her head with an arrogant gesture. 'Or very ambitious, especially if she has a nameless child to provide for. Some women would go to quite some lengths to secure a large estate for a penniless—'

'I am warning you not to use that word, *signora*.' Carol stepped with sudden decision towards Bedelia and took her by the arm. 'If we must discuss my son, then we'll do it where he won't be awoken by our voices. There is a small *salottino* just at the top of that small flight of stairs and we can talk there.'

With determination Carol drew Bedelia towards the flight of iron-railed spiral stairs that led upwards to a small room with charming antique furniture painted with cupids and garlands. Chairs of *petit-point*, a Venetian lantern at the centre of the ceiling, a writing-table with carvings of fauns dancing, and in a niche of the mimosa-coloured walls a Madonna softly lighted by a little sanctuary lamp. Carol had glanced up the stairs earlier on, but this was the first time she had actually seen the little sitting-room, and she found it so delightful that some of her disquiet was lessened as she faced Vincenzo's wife.

'I know you must have cared deeply for Vincenzo,' she said, in a gentler voice, 'and I do understand your resentment of me. But can't you try and accept Teri? He's a nice little boy, even if I do say it, and he won't understand if you resent him.'

'You are just interlopers here,' Bedelia insisted. 'You

are going to cash in on the child's resemblance to Vincenzo, that is obvious.'

'I wouldn't quite put it that way,' Carol argued, 'but I see nothing wrong in assuring for Teri a secure future, one that would have been beyond my own meagre resources. He is a Falcone, and the *baróne* isn't a poor man. I want nothing myself, *signora*, and I shall be working for my bed and board at the *palazzo*.'

'Working?' Bedelia looked astounded. 'At what, may I ask?'

'I am going to take care of the *baróne*'s library. I felt sure a house of this size and background would have a proportionate library and I used to work among books when I – I met Vincenzo.'

'Met him and chased after him, no doubt.' There was flame in the Latin eyes. 'So you were a working girl and obviously inferior to him from the very start. I have never had to work for my living. I brought a dowry to the house of Falcone, a very substantial one, and I am entitled to live here. But you—'

'I am Teri's mother,' Carol said deliberately, but keeping her eyes from that limpid gaze of the Madonna in her niche. 'I bring him instead of money, a living child who didn't ask to be born but who certainly deserves to be loved. As I warned you, *signora*, I won't tolerate any unkindness towards him – it isn't his fault that he's my son instead of yours.'

Bedelia caught her breath sharply, and though Carol didn't usually resort to being hurtful, she was fighting for Teri and she didn't want for him at Falconetti the same attitude of the Aunts at Chalkleigh, that he shouldn't have been born and didn't belong here or there.

'Do you imagine I'm jealous of *you*?' The Latin nostrils were taut with dislike and temper. 'You're just a cheap little gold-digger who lived in sin with *my* husband!'

'Thanks,' said Carol. 'That is putting it succinctly, I must say. You are welcome to make digs at me, if it gives you any satisfaction, but I promise to claw your eyes out if you harm a hair of that boy's head. He's all I care about in the world and I'll protect him like a tigress if I have to.'

Bedelia stared at the sudden blaze of Carol's eyes, matching the very colour of her wrapper. The almond-shaped Italian eyes narrowed and the pale ringed hands curled into claws against the long silken skirt of her dress. 'Yes,' she almost hissed, 'it would amuse the *baróne* to throw together in one house the two women who loved his brother. There is a side to him that is cruel and twisted as his face, English Miss. Did you know that, or did you really imagine that he was being *kind* to you?'

'Not for one moment,' Carol replied, and it struck her that there could be an element of truth in Bedelia's statement. He would realize at once that Vincenzo's childless and deserted wife would hate her, and it might indeed amuse him to watch two women at each other's throats. He must hate women in his heart and enjoy in subtle ways their unhappiness or humiliation.

Bedelia stood there glaring at Carol, pain and passion marring the face that at first sight had struck

78

Carol as being rather beautiful.

'It is as well for you to know that Rudolph isn't a kind man.'

'He's like a Roman of old,' Carol said quietly. 'I gathered that much for myself, *signora*, for knowing one Falcone has taught me that a streak of wilful passion runs in all of them.'

'And that will include your son, won't it!'

'When he grows into a man, perhaps, but right now he's a small boy and I do my best to teach him unselfishness.'

'Rudolph Falcone might teach him other things – dare you risk that?' The question was asked in a derisive and contemptuous voice. 'Perhaps that is why he wants your son to reside here, so he can take him in hand and make of him the sort of son to break a mother's heart. What a revenge for a man who has every cause to hate the very sight of a woman, especially one with blonde hair.'

'W – What do you mean by that, *signora*?' Carol felt the thump that her heart gave, one of fear and misgiving.

'Oh, didn't you know? Haven't you been told of his love affair with the singer whom he met while on a visit to his sister in America? The singer came to Rome to appear in a season of Wagner operas ... the perfect Brunnhilde with her golden hair!'

At this revelation Carol could only stare at Bedelia with the shock registering in her eyes. She had somehow taken it for granted that the *baróne* had been hurt by a fiery Latin woman, and now she was told that a golden-haired singer had caused those fearful scars. And because of that it seemed a more deliberate act of cruelty . . . a singer from New York would surely be a more sophisticated woman than a lovely, passionate, quick-tempered Latin, driven by some primitive impulse to hurt her lover.

'I would be careful of him if I were you.' Bedelia's red lips curled around the words, enjoying their menace. 'His feelings towards a woman of your colouring must be vicious, and I know if I were in your shoes I would pack my belongings and get out of his way. Of course, you could leave the child here if you are so concerned that he should have the same upbringing that Vincenzo had.'

Leave Teri to the uncertain mercies of the Falcone clan! Carol thought not, and neither would she be frightened into running away. She looked around the *salottino* and saw its charming comfort and its niched Madonna painted blue and gold.

'You can't frighten me away,' she told Bedelia. 'I know it's what you'd like to do, but I'm on my guard against your resentment.'

'Be sure you are on guard against the *baróne*'s hatred of your sort. He was always a ruthless man, and now he has cause to be a cruel one – especially when he looks at you with your pale golden hair.'

'You're making him out a devil just to suit your own purposes,' Carol said, but there went through her body a shiver of apprehension when she thought of him touching her hair and running his eyes over it as the acid-sweet memories were evoked for him.

'Make no mistake, English Miss, he can be a devil, and you are a fool if you choose to think otherwise. The Falcones trace their ancestry way back into the past, to decadent Rome, to the Borgias, to the Sabine ravishments. He was born here in this *palazzo,* was educated among the learned monks of a Benedictine Abbey, and as a young man he served as an officer in the army of an Emir – just for the fun of it. He's clever and quite fearless, but he's hard. And what that woman did to him has made him even harder, in body and heart. Beware of him – he'll take your son and break you!'

'I – I won't listen to your nonsense,' Carol gasped, backing away from the hatred she saw in Bedelia's eyes. 'You're out to frighten me just for the hell of it.'

'It's interesting that you speak of hell.' Bedelia slowly smiled, but without a hint of humour in her eyes. 'We all pass through it, one way or another, don't we?'

She turned away with these words and as she went down the spiral stairs her laughter floated back to Carol, infinitely mocking, and all the more nerveracking because it was unstable. Vincenzo's desertion had cut deeply into Bedelia's heart because she had probably loved him as Carol hadn't.

Carol's hands clenched together ... she had been swept into an infatuation by the Italian charm of Vincenzo Falcone, and it had died in that moment when she had caught him with Cynara in his arms. Cynara, her own bridesmaid at a wedding which had been as false as Vincenzo's declaration of love for her.

Love . . . she was a girl *désenchantée* in the house of a man with every reason to hate a woman with long blonde hair.

The future loomed ahead of Carol like the big bedroom to which she returned . . . a future filled with terrifying uncertainties. With half her mind and heart she wanted to take flight and leave Falconetti, but with the more spirited side of herself she wanted the advantages that being a member of this family would provide for Teri. She couldn't face the thought of returning to Chalkleigh and a renewal of their life with the Aunts, and at the same time she was daunted by an image of their life in one of the poorer parts of Rome, where Teri would go to a rundown school and spend hours in the streets with ragamuffin children while she worked in some café as a waitress or a kitchen help.

Almost unaware, she sank into a kneeling position beside the great bed where Teri slept so soundly and her bright hair spread around her as she rested her forehead against the silk and lace coverlet. It was cool against her hot forehead and the jabbing pain of a headache. She had said defiantly that Bedelia didn't frighten her with her remarks about the *baróne*, but it wasn't altogether true.

He could be every bit as untrustworthy as Vincenzo, and added to it he carried those terrible marks, as if a tigress had leapt and clawed his face into the mask of a devil.

According to Bedelia it wasn't just a mask, and try as she might Carol couldn't quite believe that 'the damned are not forever lost'.

CHAPTER FOUR

CAROL woke abruptly to a flood of sunlight through the long windows, from which the curtains had been pulled aside into graceful drapes to the polished floor. She lay there gazing bemusedly at the sunshine and the enormous windows that let it into the room. Where on earth ... then she sat up sharply as the door of the strange room opened and a maid in a cream and beige uniform entered with a tray in her hands.

'*Buon giorno, signora.*' The maid came to the bedside and the wink of silver made Carol blink. Never in her life had she been brought tea in bed, least of all in a silver pot by a young maid in an impeccable uniform.

'Good morning,' she said, and then she remembered exactly where she was and turned in panic to find Teri. The place beside her was empty and only the slight impression of his young head remained in the pillow.

'Teri!' she gasped. 'Where is he?'

'I came earlier with tea, *signora*, but you were sound asleep and the *bambino* was wide awake. He wanted to get up and have a look around, and the *padrina* said it would be all right.'

'The *padrina*?' Carol looked perplexed and anxious for Teri.

'The sister of the *padrone, signora*. She is an early riser and she took the *bambino* off with her.'

'Oh – Gena.' Relief came into Carol's eyes. 'Is it

very late? I don't usually sleep so deeply.'

'It is nine-thirty, *signora*, but do not worry yourself. The *padrona* said that you were not to be disturbed, but I thought you might wish for a cup of tea and I have brought it to you.'

'I'd love a cup!' Carol pushed aside her thick plait that was half-unwound, a sign that her sleep had been restless for all that she had slept so deeply. The sun played upon her and she could feel the maid looking at her with a hint of curiosity, taking in her blonde hair as she poured tea from the silver pot into a porcelain cup. 'There is cream and sugar, *signora*, and a second cup in the pot. Will you take breakfast here in your room, or down on the *terrazza*?'

'Oh, the *terrazza* sounds ideal,' Carol said at once.

'And what will the *signora* require for breakfast? Fruit and rolls, or something a little more substantial?'

'A half of grapefruit would be nice, followed by bacon and toast if that wouldn't be too much bother?'

'Not at all, *signora*.' The maid looked faintly amused that a guest should be so polite. 'You may have bacon and eggs, a slice of fish, buttered waffles and cream—'

'Teri would love those,' Carol said eagerly. 'He has a very sweet tooth and he dashes about such a lot that he could do with a little fattening up.'

'*Si, signora*. Breakfast will be brought to you on the *terrazza* at any time that pleases you. It will be nice having a *bambino* in the house, and he does indeed seem a very lively little boy.'

'When he was younger and I took him shopping I had to put reins on him,' Carol smiled. 'I – I daresay

84

the staff have heard that he is the son of the Signore Vincenzo?'

The maid nodded. 'The likeness is there, *signora*.'

'I hope everyone is not too scandalized.' Carol tried to speak lightly, for it would have to be faced that she would be thought of as Vincenzo's mistress.

'We are the servants of the *baróne* and we don't presume to make judgments, *signora*.' The maid ran her gaze over Carol's pensive face and silky hair, falling undone around her slim and vulnerable-looking shoulders. 'The Signore Vincenzo was extremely handsome, and it is some consolation for the family that he left a son. These things happen. Life is life.'

After the maid was gone, Carol was left with the feeling that life at Falconetti might not be too hard to take ... so long as these people went on regarding her as the mother of Teri. They could forgive what they thought of as a sexual transgression, but if it came out that she was lying to them about having given birth to a Falcone child, then she felt no doubt about their reaction.

Her darling Teri would be taken from her, and when she remembered him as a toddler in those red and yellow knitted reins, she could hardly bear to think of being parted from him.

Her hands clenched around her cup of tea ... the deception must go on for all it was worth, and the best way for her to handle it was to think of it as an adventure. There had been few of those in her life, least of all in surroundings such as these.

That sunshine! Her eyes glistened at the golden

warmth and all at once she felt a longing to be out in it and she quickly finished her tea and went to the bathroom.

Half an hour later she was ready to go down to the *terrazza* and outside her apartment she paused on the gallery to catch the sound of Teri's voice. It floated on a laugh through an open door at the corner of the gallery, an arched door that gave it the appearance of a hideaway, and Carol went towards it and looked inside. Teri was there with Gena and Flavia, and they had cupboards open in the room and an assortment of toys and games were strewn about the floor. There was also a big dolls' house, a highly-painted rocking-horse, and a big clown sitting in a Neptune chair.

'There you are,' she said, entering the room, and smiling at the bright disorder of toy soldiers, toy trains and their tracks, and Gena in a silk wrap holding a big doll in her arms.

'Hi there,' said Gena. 'We're investigating our old playroom for toys that Teri might like to play with. These soldiers belonged to Rudi – aren't they terrific? Handmade and perfect in every detail.'

'Look at this, Cally.' Teri ran to her with a Roman soldier complete with helmet, shield and sword. 'I've never seen soldiers like these before, and Zia Gena says they're centurions of Caesar's army. May I play with them?'

'Of course you may, and how about a good morning kiss?' Carol bent down to him and very solemnly they kissed each other. She could feel Gena giving them an intent look and when she glanced across the room she was really feeling a lot less composed than she looked, with her hair neatly braided and wearing a slim green skirt and a white and green polka-dot shirt.

'It's kind of you both to do this for Teri,' she said. 'It's a regular treasure trove for him to explore, but I hope your brother won't mind? Those soldiers look as if they've been well cared for, and I'd hate Teri to break one of them.'

'Rudi has long outgrown these kind of toys,' Gena drawled. 'Teri is welcome to use the playroom and he might as well call the soldiers and trains his very own, for there aren't likely to be any more children to play with them.'

'Oh, why do you say that?' Carol studied Gena in the ivory-coloured wrap, sitting there on a velvet hammock with the doll cradled against her. 'I'm sure your brother doesn't expect you to remain a spinster.'

'I rather expect it of myself, because I fall for heels.' Gena grinned and glanced at Flavia. 'And you, pet, you want to take the veil, eh?'

Flavia smiled shyly. 'If Papa is agreeable, of course. The nuns who taught us were always so serene and I feel drawn towards the order and discipline of the life. You wouldn't understand, Gena.'

'You can take a bet on that and be sure of winning.' Gena rose to her feet and tossed aside the doll. 'I had better go and dress myself, and you, honey, can take Carol and her boy down to breakfast. I expect they're ravenous – yes, lamb chop,' she addressed Teri, 'you can take the Roman commander with you. You've taken to that fierce-looking guy, haven't you?'

87

Teri nodded and studied the soldier. 'Was the tall man wounded in a war?' he asked. 'Did a tank run over him?'

'Yes, *caro mio*, I daresay you could call it a battle, only it wasn't a tank that he tangled with. Tell me,' Gena bent down to Teri and held his chin in her hand, 'you aren't frightened of the tall man, are you?'

Teri shook his head. 'I don't think so, Zia Gena. Does it hurt him?'

'Only when people act silly and treat him as if he frightens them. He was once as handsome as a real Roman centurion and all sorts of people used to lick his boots. Sometimes he'll seem not to be aware of you, *mio*, and you mustn't mind, for he gets lost in his thoughts and has moods when he wants to be all alone. You see, little man, he no longer believes that anyone can love him.'

Teri thought this over, and then glanced round at Carol as if assuring himself that she was there with the soft love in her eyes that never wavered.

'Feeling hungry, Buster?' she asked him.

He nodded and walked between Carol and the *baróne*'s adopted daughter as they went down the wide marble stairs to the lower hall and out through one of the elegant arched doorways on to a wide terrace overlooking the lake.

In the morning sunlight the water glittered as if strewn with silver pieces and in an instant Teri was leaning over the parapet, his legs half off the ground. Flavia started forward in some alarm, but Carol caught at her arm. 'Come along, Buster,' she said, 'I

88

don't want a ducking if you fall in and I have to fetch you out. You know what hours it takes for my hair to dry, and I have work to do.'

'Work?' He swung round from the parapet. 'What, in a teashop?'

'No, here in the *palazzo*. I'm going to mend books and earn my bread and butter. Look, *caro*, here comes the maid with your waffles and cream.'

He came at once to the table, grinning at Flavia as he wriggled his way on to his iron-wrought chair with a cushioned seat. 'What are they?' he asked.

'They're like little pancakes, only they aren't folded,' she told him.

'Goodie!' He stood his Roman soldier against the plaited basket in which rolls were laid. Then he looked about him, wrinkling his nostrils. 'I can smell lemons, Cally. Lots and lots of lemons.'

'There is a lemon house close by,' Flavia said. 'Would you like to see it when you've had your breakfast?'

'A house made of lemons?' He stared at her in amazed delight.

'No, *caro*, not exactly that. It is a big cool place where we store the lemons after they have been plucked from the trees.'

'It would have been funny, a house made of lemons.' He grinned, and then transferred his attention to the maid as she laid out the various dishes of bacon, waffles scrambled eggs, and fruit. The maid gave him a frank stare, and Carol could see for herself that Teri's Italian look was intensified in these surroundings. Vincenzo had certainly imposed his looks upon his son, and Carol had to be thankful for it despite her misgivings. It acted like a charm and made the situation more piquant than uncomfortable.

She leaned across to Teri and poured the golden cream on to his waffles, which he proceeded to eat with boyish relish. She smiled a little to herself and served her own plate with bacon and tomatoes, while Flavia ate sparingly of scrambled egg. She was a nice girl, but so reserved that Carol found it difficult making small talk with her. Her mind seemed miles away, as if she already saw herself at peace among the cloisters of the convent, saved from the kind of tensions that came into the lives of men and women who preferred the emotions of the heart rather than the soul.

'Will you mind leaving such a beautiful part of the country?' she asked, after a while. 'The *palazzo* and the lake appear to have great interest and beauty, and I'm afraid I am worldly enough to feel daunted by the mere thought of entering a nunnery.'

Flavia smiled gently with her big brown eyes. 'I feel no doubts at all about taking holy orders,' she replied. 'The need to do so is there in my heart, and I feel that everyone should follow their own chosen star. I shall train to be a nurse and be of good use to the Order, for it isn't an enclosed one. I think I should like to go out to India later on, where is a great deal of suffering among the very poor people.'

'I think you're very brave,' Carol said, sincerely. 'But you're also very young—'

'Only in years,' Flavia murmured. 'There is wickedness in the world, and there must be people to fight it if they can. I find the prospect far more exciting than settling down to family life with a husband.'

'Yet you're a very pretty girl,' Carol told her. 'Will the *baróne* be happy with your desire to take the veil?'

'He will understand. He has always been kind to me, and I know that he wants me to be happy.'

'What is the veil?' Teri suddenly asked, for even in the midst of enjoying his food Carol had learned long ago that he was intrigued by the talk of grown up people. The Aunts had found his questions impudent and had insisted that he and Carol eat separately. She hadn't minded that, but it had annoyed her that his youthful curiosity should be regarded as offensive to anyone. He was naturally forward and Carol had always ensured that he didn't cheek people.

'I am going to work for God,' Flavia told him, with her gentle smile. 'He will be my Boss and I shall take orders from Him, and my uniform will be a veil.'

'Can I wear one when I'm all grown up?' he wanted to know. 'Though I think I would like to be a soldier and fight wars.'

'What a bloodthirsty young man!' drawled a deep voice, and Carol turned a startled head to find the *baróne* halfway along the *terrazza*, his strides in high brown boots so long that he reached their table almost before she could catch her breath. He wore well-weathered breeches and a cambric shirt, and he had a look of sardonic hauteur as he paused there against the stone lace of the parapet, his boots planted on the mosaic paving.

He and Teri stared at each other in the morning sunlight that revealed so cruelly the destroyed half of the *baróne*'s face. His falcon gold eyes searched every inch of the childish face raised to him, and Carol saw him shake his head in a sort of wonderment, and she knew that he was remembering his brother and seeing him again in Teri's face and eyes.

'Have you been riding, sir?' Teri asked him, staring at the hefty boots and the whip in the brown hand. 'I saw your big black horse and he made steam come out of his nostrils.'

'Caliph is high-tempered and knows he's the lord of my stables. So you like horses, eh?'

'And monkeys,' Teri replied. 'Have you any of those, sir?'

'I am your *zio*, young man. No, we haven't any monkeys here apart from yourself.'

Instinctively a smile caught at Carol's lips ... so a certain humour was lurking behind that dark, scarred and rather haughty mask? She relaxed just a little, for she had been dreading the thought that he might be stern towards Teri; a sort of ogre who would frighten the boy. But it seemed that he could be quite human, when it suited him.

'I'm not a monkey,' Teri informed him, with great gravity. 'I'm a boy.'

At once, Carol noticed, those deep lines beside the man's mouth seemed to soften slightly. 'You are much like your father when he was a boy,' he said. 'He always had a taste for sweet things, and I see that you take after him in that. Your son is not a finicky eater.

madam.' He transferred his gaze so swiftly to Carol that he caught her staring at him; at once she felt the heat rising from the neck of her shirt and flowing over her face in a blush that would have been worthy of a schoolgirl. His eyes derided her for the blush, she felt sure of that, but she strove not to look away from him.

'Teri has had to learn, *signore*, that food has to be worked for and costs money. He's a good boy in that respect.'

'Is he always a good boy?' A black brow rode up against his dark skin, and she could tell that he knew how painfully vivid were the acid burns in the full play of sunlight along the *terrazza*.

'He's no angel, *signore*, but I've taught him a few values. He is a Falcone, after all.'

'Indisputably.' Again the *baróne* looked at Teri, who now had half his face in a mug of chocolate. 'You have done a good job, madam, for a young woman left on her own to cope. What made you suddenly come to us when you are obviously not the sort to like charity?'

'I hope you don't regard it as charity, *signore*.' She felt suddenly stung by him, as if he had flicked at her skin with his whip. 'I wanted Teri to have a place in the sun. Is that so very wrong of – of a mother of a son?'

'Commendable,' he drawled. 'Love should rise above pride, but one would like to know why it took five years. Did you learn suddenly that the Falcones were affluent?'

He had asked her that yesterday and had seemed to accept her explanation, but she supposed that it would strike him as odd that she should suddenly turn up like

93

this with a five-year-old son. She was a woman, and he had learned the painful way not to trust a member of her sex.

She tried not to be resentful of his distrust, but it certainly took an effort. Perhaps in the clarity of daylight he saw himself as a man taken in, and resented it. Hadn't Gena said that he was still warm-blooded enough to respond to a new face at the *palazzo*? A man *désenchanté* but still very much a man in his riding boots laced with strips of leather, his breeches fitting firm against his flat stomach, and his shirt fine enough to show the shadow of a dark-haired chest. She caught the whisper of his whip as he moved it against the sunlit stone, and she saw the gleam of an onyx ring on his hand; a large gem that she had felt against her skin when he had touched her last night.

Suddenly Flavia gave a giggle and pointed at Teri, who sat there with a chocolate moustache and looked comical. 'Buster, do wipe your mouth,' Carol said, 'no, not on the back of your hand but on your napkin. That's better. Did you enjoy your breakfast?'

'Smashing,' he said. 'Can I get down from the table, Cally?'

'Yes, if you've quite finished.'

He slid from his chair and approached the *baróne*, who towered above him in the sunlight. Suddenly the man bent and lifted the boy to the parapet and sat him there with a firm brown arm around him. In his hand Teri had the Roman soldier, and the *baróne* quirked his eyebrow as he caught sight of it.

'They were my favourite playthings,' he said. 'Did

you know that I was once a soldier?'

'Were you really, *zio*?' Teri stared frankly at the scarred side of his uncle's face. 'You got that fighting, didn't you? Were you very brave? It must have hurt ever such a lot.'

Carol held her breath, as she invariably did when Teri referred to that fearful distortion of a once handsome face; a face such as the boy's would be when he reached manhood. The Falcone face, with the ferocious splendour of a Roman nose, and 'an eye like Mars to threaten and command', and a mouth in which strength mingled with a certain sensuality.

'Physical pain can be borne, *bràvo*. See down on the lake that boat with the scarlet sails? That belongs to me and one afternoon we will go sailing, eh? All the way round the island, which is a fairly large one.'

Teri caught his breath in delight. 'Cally, I'm going sailing!' he called out, leaning far out over the lake in the crook of a steel-like arm. 'I'm so glad we came here, Cally, and I don't want to ever go away again.'

'The call of the blood,' drawled Gena as she came along the *terrazza*, clad in a red shirt and a pair of ivory-coloured breeches. 'I'll have a cup of coffee, and then I'm off for a gallop. Can I take Domino, Rudi? I know she was out of temper with me the other day, but only because a snake crossed our path. She'll be fine today and won't attempt to break my precious neck.'

'Be less reckless, Gena,' her brother said, with just the faintest edge of steel to his voice. 'It isn't always necks that snap, it's backbones, and you would find it intolerable to be helpless and dependent upon the

95

patience of other people.'

'Don't!' She gave a mock shudder and winked at Teri over the rim of her coffee cup. 'I see, *caro*, that you're keeping high and mighty company. My dear Rudi, I do believe the boy is more like you than Vince himself.'

'Then you must have X-ray eyes, my dear sister.' The *baróne* spoke with sudden curtness and swung Teri to the ground. 'Run along with Flavia and get to know your new home, for you are now the young *signorino* and what is ours is yours.'

Words that were music to Carol's ears, for she knew they were sincere and would not be repudiated by Rudolph Falcone, no matter what he found out about her. Her position was vulnerable and he was capable of hurting her very badly, but Teri was secure and that was the most important thing of all. Secure as a Falcone despite the illegitimacy of his birth, because the *baróne* said so and his word was law on the *isola*.

'You will come with me, madam.' He reached down and drew Carol to her feet, clasping her elbow with firm fingers. She obeyed him because she had no option, and she heard Gena give a low laugh.

'You, sister,' he said, 'will take care of your own neck and that of the mare's. Understood?'

'*Si, signore*.' She swept him a slight bow. 'If I see Saul Stern, may I ask him to dine tonight, so he can meet our fair visitor? I say, look at her hair in the sun! Blonde as Lucrezia, isn't she?'

Even as Gena said this, she bit her lip. It might at times slip her mind that a blonde had disfigured her brother, but it could never fade from his mind, and his fingers seemed to dig into Carol's arm as he led her along the *terrazza* and down a flight of stone steps, across a garden court surrounded by flowers and shrubs, and with a walled lily pool at its centre. There was a spiral of stairs at the end of the court, with a scrolled railing leading up to a medieval-looking tower whose narrow windows must have looked far out along the lake.

'It's all right,' the *baróne* drawled, when Carol pulled back slightly from the stairs. 'I'm taking you to my drawing-room, not to my private torture chamber. I want to talk to you, and everyone has instructions not to disturb me in this part of the house. This is the oldest wing, the *scala del falconiere* where an ancestor of mine kept his hunting birds. Come, it has a fine view, and one can imagine him letting the falcons fly out after the pigeons.'

'How cruel,' she said, but she preceded him up the stairs and was acutely aware of him following on behind, those falcon eyes of his on her legs. The stairs led straight to a thick arched door, and Carol stood aside for him to open it. She looked around with amazement, for the room was adorned, if that was the word, by strange creatures and gargoyles. A Murano glass lantern hung from the ceiling, its framework of black iron, and against one white wall there hung a large painting of a monk in medieval hood and habit. Carol stared, for the eyes that looked out of the dark stern face were the golden eyes of Rudolph Falcone.

'My ancestor who liked falcons,' he said. 'He wasn't part of a holy sect, but he liked to dress in that manner.

He was more unholy than anything else, so it is said.'

'The eyes,' she gasped, 'they seem alive!'

'Don't they?' He closed the heavy door and stood there looking at her, and to avoid his eyes she added to her impressions of the room by studying the tall kingwood cabinets that held an assortment of books, topped by falcons in carved wood, a menacing look to the way they peered downward, their beaks and claws cruelly distinct.

Over by a window there was a drawing-stand such as artists or architects might use, and Carol recalled what Gena had said about the *baróne*, that he designed the engines for motor-boats and racing-cars. Yes, she thought, he would want an occupation, for there was something alert and active in his every glance and movement. It wouldn't suit such a man to live the idle life of a wealthy aristocrat, and when he saw her looking at the drawing-board he said, sardonically:

'Yes, I too like to work for my bed and board, madam. It doesn't entirely suit me to live on the looted treasures of this house, though I certainly admit to finding pleasure in their beauty.'

As he spoke that final word his eyes dwelt on Carol's hair, the coloured upper panels of the gothic windows playing over its fairness and creating a sort of nimbus.

She tensed and wondered what was going through his mind. Did the look of her make him remember with painful – no, agonizing vividness that terrible moment when the acid had struck his face, flung at him by a woman mad with love or hate?

Love could be terrible . . . terrible as hate if a woman

could be driven to such an act.

'Won't you take a seat, madam?' He gestured to a deep chair that seemed to be covered in a thick dull material like monk's cloth. As Carol sat down she wondered if this man had taken to a sort of monk's life since having his face and heart burned by acid.

He didn't sit down himself but went to lean against one of the purplish-brown book cabinets, a carved falcon peering down at his black head, and so placed that he was out of range of the sunlight through the peaked windows. 'Have you thought, madam, that while your son is a child he will have the protection of his family's love? Have you realized that when he goes away to school there will be those who will regard him as unentitled to his father's name?'

Her hands clenched the arms of her chair, for his words seemed to shaft into her like so many painful arrows. 'Yes,' she said quietly, 'I've thought about it, now I – now I know that Vincenzo had a wife before he – he met me. I know that some people can be – spiteful, and Teri is such a knowing child that he will be susceptible to the barbed remarks. One of the reasons I wanted to get him away from my aunts was their attitude that he—' Carol bit her lip. 'They are old-fashioned in their outlook on life, and they thought that Teri should not have been born.'

'And why should they take such an attitude when you believed yourself to be the legal wife of my brother?'

Carol gazed across at him and saw from his frown that she was skating on thin and dangerous ice. 'He was

99

dead, *signore*, and it's always hard for a child to be brought up by a single parent.'

'Indeed, and that brings me to the point of this discussion. A growing boy should have a father, and most certainly a name. I have decided that you will become my wife, madam.'

'What?' Carol stared at him as if he had suggested that she leap from the tower window. 'Y-you can't be serious!'

'I am deadly serious, madam. The boy is a Falcone and I wish him to have the full protection of my name and my position.'

'Marriage!' she gasped. 'It's out of the question!'

'It's very much part of the question,' he said, and his voice was as firm as steel. 'If you become my wife, then your son becomes my son, and no one will dare to breathe a word of scandal in connection with the boy, unless they wish to deal with me. I can be a harsh man when angered, madam.'

'I don't doubt it,' she said, and could feel her heart beating so hard that she might have been running, and indeed she felt as if she were running madly away in her mind from this mad and impossible proposal of marriage from a man she hardly knew. He was Vincenzo's brother and she had learned to distrust any hint of Latin charm and persuasion . . . not that there was anything that remotely resembled charm in the *baróne*'s attitude at this precise moment. His eyes were a hard, demanding gold that intensified the dark, scarred nobility of his face.

'If you don't doubt it, then don't make me angry,' he

said. 'As a Falcone I'm not proud of the fact that my brother led you up a garden path strewn with thorns. I can make reparation for that, and you will permit me to do so.'

Carol sat there stunned, and up through the windows floated the sound of cicadas grating their back legs in the foliage of the gardens. She smelled the heady musk of flowers mingling with that of old stone and water. 'I – I could never agree to such a reparation,' she said at last. 'You have no need to go that far, *signore*, for two people you knew nothing about until we turned up on your doorstep.'

'You are looking for excuses,' he said, with a sudden touch of harshness. 'You declare your love for the boy, but it isn't strong enough to make you close your eyes to the face of a ugly husband. Did you imagine, madam, that I was proposing a love match, and that I'd expect you to fall into my arms?'

'Yes – no–' Carol didn't know what she expected, certainly not a proposal of any sort from a powerful Italian landowner. 'Surely you didn't expect me to say yes to you?'

'Am I such a monster?' he asked.

'Oh no – your face has nothing to do with it! We're strangers to each other, that's what I meant. You don't owe Teri that much, to tie yourself to – to your brother's woman.'

'You requested that I didn't call you his woman, but others will do so. Though you live under my roof, there will be whispers about your son. Are you strong enough to take those, but not brave enough to marry me?'

Strong enough? Her hands trembled, and she was so tired of being tough all the time, afraid to give in to weakness and tears. For five years she had stood alone and fought for Teri, but now – now a man offered to share that burden and it would have been terribly tempting to just give in and not fight any more.

'Strangers don't marry, *signore*,' she said. 'I made that mistake once before, and I daren't make it again, least of all with Vincenzo's very own brother.'

'Do you imagine I am like him? Women were a relaxation for me, not an obsession. It was another woman, I suppose, who took Vincenzo away from you?'

'Yes.' She saw Cynara again, so defiant, with smeared lips, and a rip in her violet-coloured brides-maid's dress.

'You wouldn't be entirely the type of woman for my brother.' Those eyes that might never soften again for any woman made a relentless search of Carol's face. 'I never knew him to go in for the sensitive type with a mind of her own, but at eighteen you would have been as tender and untouched as a new rose, and I imagine he found that irresistible – for a while. Then he reverted to the more obvious sort, am I correct?'

'Uncannily correct,' she said, and it gave her a curious jolt that this man should speak of her as an untouched rose ... how did he regard her now, as a fallen flower?

'What I have proposed must be decided one way or the other,' he said. 'Come, you aren't a starry-eyed girl any more, looking from your virgin casement for a knight on horseback. You and I have in common our disillusion with the delights of love, and we can regard marriage as a mere business arrangement. I can give your son the name that he should have, so that it can never be disputed, and you can give me the heir that I wouldn't have in the normal course of events. You see, madam, I don't expect a woman to love my face. I look at it in a mirror each morning when I shave and I would be a fool to expect anything but pity and a certain horror from any young woman. That I would never deliberately seek, and you can rest assured that I would be but a husband in name alone.'

Carol sat there as still as a statue, but she could actually feel the excitement running in her veins. Teri could be this man's heir, with a title and a *palazzo*, and people looking up to him. The sin of Cynara could be wiped out as if it had never been, and the child she loved could hold his own with anyone . . . just about anyone.

Abruptly the *baróne* leaned down to her and looked closely into her eyes. 'Yes, now the idea spreads wings and you feel yourself being carried away by what I suggest. Never again need you worry about your son's future . . . or your own, come to that. You are tempted, are you not?'

'Yes,' she admitted. 'But all the same it's a cold-blooded arrangement, and even if I don't have to be your real wife, how can I be sure that I won't be your hated wife?'

'Why should I hate you?' There was the faintest hint of whimsicality in his voice. 'I shall probably take you for granted, for I have my own life to live, my own concerns that keep me well occupied.'

'I – I know how you became as you are,' she said, and she looked at him though it would have been infinitely easier to glance away, at the falcons that couldn't fly, at that monk-like figure whose eyes couldn't play tricks with her nerves.

'Do you really, madam?' His voice was velvet wrapped around a shaft of steel, and his glance flicked like the sharp point of the rapier. 'Is that why you're afraid of marrying me?'

'Being hurt in that way can't make you exactly fond of – of women.'

'Of blonde women?' he taunted her, and quite deliberately he touched a tendril of soft gold hair at the side of her neck. She felt the very tip of his finger and tiny nerves seemed to chase each other across the very pit of her stomach.

'How can I tell that you don't want some kind of – revenge?' she said. 'It wouldn't be unnatural, and once I became your wife – well, you're the *baróne*, and no one questions your authority, do they?'

'Meaning that if I beat you there would be no one to tell me that I shouldn't?'

'Something like that.'

'What an odd creature you are!' He flung back his head and gave a hard sort of laugh. 'You'd be more likely to scream if I made love to you.'

When he said that Carol very nearly did scream; married to him she would have little defence against anything that he wished to do. He was a hard, lean, powerful man, and forever branded by the cruelty of a woman. There would be no tenderness in the love-making of Rudolph Falcone, and she was not the experienced woman that she made out to be.

'You know you can't fight me,' he said, 'so why bother to try? You know you would do almost any-thing for the boy—'

And there he broke off as the door of the tower room was abruptly thrust open, framing the figure of Bedelia Falcone, clad in dark silk that glistened like her eyes and her drawn-back hair. In the lobes of her ears were black pearls gleaming against the magnolia pallor of her skin.

'I thought I would find the pair of you together.' Her pale, long-fingered hands curled against the silk of her dress. 'I guessed that *she* wouldn't waste much time before she started her wiles on yet another Falcone, and this time the rich, important one. I said that was why she came here, and I am proved right. You bring no one here, Rudolph, so she followed you—'

'Mrs. Adams did nothing of the sort,' he said, curtly. 'I brought her with me to the *falconiere,* and I had my reason for doing so.'

'Your reason?' Bedelia flung back her head and gave him an arrogant look. 'Of course, you realize that she is no better than a woman of the streets and you feel she should repay you for being here.'

'How dare you!' Carol went white with temper and sprang to her feet. 'I'm not taking your insults—'

'You will be quiet, the pair of you,' the *baróne* rapped out. 'There will be no cat fights under my roof, do you hear? Women! Life would so much more composed if they had never been invented.'

'Why is she here?' Bedelia demanded. 'Here in your private room from which others of the household are excluded.'

'Mrs. Adams and I had something of a serious nature to discuss.'

'Money?' his sister-in-law flung at him. 'Is she demanding a settlement of some sort, so she can dress her little mistake in better clothes than the ones he is wearing at present? Cheap people, cheaply dressed! How could Vincenzo get mixed up with her sort when he was used to the best?'

'Hold your tongue.' The *baróne* looked so suddenly angry that his scars stood out like pale frozen seams. 'You are speaking of the woman who is going to be my wife!'

Bedelia looked at him as if he had gone mad, then all at once her hands were claws and she was flying straight at Carol, her sharp fingernails aimed at her eyes. Carol gave a cry and then felt herself falling as the *baróne* thrust her to one side and caught hold of Bedelia with incredible speed and strength. He gave her a shake that must have rattled her teeth.

'What is the matter with you?' he demanded. 'Are you deranged?'

'You can't marry her, you can't,' Bedelia panted. 'You can have the child without having her – she is nothing, and you are the *baróne*. Give her money and she will go away, Rudolph. That is all she came for, to be paid for having the son that should have been mine.'

'You don't know what you are saying,' he said grimly. 'Grow up, Bedelia, and find yourself another husband. Forget Vincenzo, once and for all. Accept that he is gone for good. *Che sarà sarà*.'

'I was his wife – I loved him. What is *she*? Just one of his women who fell for his child and who now comes to Falconetti to get all she can out of you. You can't marry her! People will know that she isn't doing it because she wants you! It's your possessions that she wants!'

'I am fully aware that no woman could want me for myself,' he said, and Carol saw a nerve flickering against his temple, distinct among his fearful scars. 'But as a man of property I must have a legal heir, and young Terence will suit me. He has the Falcone look, and he's healthy and intelligent beyond his years.'

Carol listened as if in a kind of dream from which she couldn't wake up. This was her future they were talking about, as if it were already settled that she was going to make the vows that would bind her to this man. She wanted to cry out that it wasn't settled, but her lips moved dumbly, as they do in dreams, and she knew in her heart that Rudolph Falcone would have his way.

He looked at her, still gripping Bedelia by the arms, and there in his eyes lay not demand but the distant expression of a man who had chosen to protect his inmost feelings with a layer of ice that marriage to her would leave as frozen as it was right now.

'We shall be married,' he said. 'Soon.'

'Yes,' she heard herself reply, and there was a long

moment of silence broken by the rustle of silk as Bedelia broke free of the *baróne*'s hands.

'You will regret what you are doing,' she flung at him, and the gems in her ears held a black fire, reflected by her eyes. 'Have you not already learned your lesson at the hands of a blonde woman!'

With this taunt Bedelia glanced around the *falconiere* until her gaze fell upon the monk-like portrait, and she flung out a hand towards it. 'You would do better to live like that, brother-in-law,' she said. 'Take to the cowl and the habit, for this cheap and pretty piece who belonged to Vincenzo isn't going to kiss you with her eyes open.'

Bedelia smiled at him, and then turned away with a catlike grace and walked from the room, and never in her life had Carol felt such a spasm of hatred for anyone.

But at the same time she felt a deep stab of curiosity ... was it possible that Bedelia spoke like that out of sheer wilful envy? Had she transferred love of her dead husband to his living brother ... The *baróne* of Falconetti who had all the strength and authority which Vincenzo had lacked?

When she looked at the *baróne* he was gazing from one of the peaked windows down upon the lake, and turned to her was the unflawed side of his face ... the face which Bedelia had known in all its Latin perfection.

Carol's heart gave a thump, for she knew that even as she gained the *baróne* for a husband, she gained a deadly enemy in his sister-in-law.

'Bedelia is highly strung,' he said, 'and she doesn't always take heed of what she says. She would have been more stable had there been a child of her union with Vincenzo – it is natural that she is jealous of your son.'

'It might be natural,' said Carol, 'but she makes me rather afraid. I hope she wouldn't harm Teri—'

'Harm him?' He swung round and looked hard at Carol. 'I hardly think so, for she knows she would have me to deal with. As I said, we shall be married as soon as possible, but there are certain formalities to arrange and papers to be drawn up. I realize that it is all very unromantic, but the advantages should outweigh the lack of – enchantment, shall I say?'

'Don't bother to say it, *signore*.' She briefly, and a little bitterly, broke into a smile. 'I am quite disenchanted with romance, and it is true that I would do just about everything for Teri. He comes first with me, and I'm grateful that you wish to make him your official heir – but please believe that I didn't come here deliberately seeking that, as Bedelia implied. I'm not a gold-digger, and neither am I a cheap woman who would give myself to any man. You said, *signore*, that our marriage would be a mere formality, but if it were that alone then I would feel that I was cheating you. If I marry you, I will be your wife, if you want me to be so.'

Carol hadn't weighed her words, or even thought that she would say them, but directly she did so she felt a sense of relief. She didn't want to take all that this man was prepared to give to Teri without some sort of repayment, and he was a lonely man ... a man who believed that he was no longer desirable; a kind of ogre to shut himself away in his *falconiere* so that other people might not have to hide the shock in their eyes when they looked at his face.

'You are generous, madam.' He stood there very tall and straight, with an old-world hauteur about him, as of another time, when men clad themselves in doublet and hose and carried a rapier at the hip.

And then he said, rather cruelly: 'But I'm not asking for your self-sacrifice, you know. It's your son that I want, to carry on my name and my line, and it is necessary that in order to acquire him in every sense of the word I marry his mother. You have no need to grit your teeth and come to bed with me, Mrs. Adams. I am not so desperate for the company of a woman that I would subject you to the embraces of a man you neither like nor want. You will be my wife in everything but the intimacy of the bedroom, for I don't require your pity, madam.'

When he said that Carol felt as if the floor rocked beneath her feet. She hated him for the way he spoke, and the way he looked at her with eyes like steel with an edge of flame to them. He was armoured in pride, and when he smiled it was remote as a moon glimmer.

He gave her a slight mocking bow. 'I salute your courage, madam. It must have taken plenty to offer yourself to a man whose looks must make you shrink inside yourself. You are young and attractive. My handsome brother was your lover. You have no need to consider yourself under any kind of obligation to me.'

'I – I didn't want you to think that I would take

without being prepared to give,' she said, in a shaken voice. She could barely meet his gaze – he mortified her, her *fidanzato*.

'It's because of my brother that you have the responsibility of a son to rear, so it's for me to do something about it. I shall be of use to you, and in return you assist me in making secure the future of this *isola* and its people. We are almost feudal on this island, madam. The people like it that they have a *baróne* to give them employment, and to whom they can bring their problems. Terence will be reared in this tradition, you realize that?'

'Yes,' she said quietly. 'If you are quite certain that you won't have a son of your own.'

'Children should be born of love or not at all.' The firm shoulders moved the cambric shirt in a shrug of great irony. 'Come to the window, madam, and take a look at what will be your son's when he inherits from me.'

Carol moved slowly to his side and she could feel a strange sort of weakness in her legs, and when she stood there beside him it just couldn't be ignored that she was consumed by a disturbing awareness of this man. She gazed down upon the shimmering lake and its surrounding landscape, and all the time she was asking herself why he should so disturb her, so that she would jump like a startled spider if he should touch her.

He spoke as if no woman would ever look at him again, yet he could have had some sort of cosmetic surgery which would have reduced the shock effect of his face. That he chose not to have the scars sewn over with plastic skin could only mean that he wanted the protection of his acid burns. He wanted from now on to keep at bay the enticement of love; he had convinced himself that no woman would come into his arms willingly.

The sun on the Lake of Lina was blindingly bright, so that the overhanging trees along its waterworn walls looked like shaggy black etchings. Hanging gardens and terraces that cast a spell over the senses. Leafy vines and masses of golden mimosa clambering over walls ... A self-contained island with the *palazzo* dominating the cluster of white houses, the lemon groves, the grapevines and the fig orchards. Espaliered fruit trees shone in the sun, the water quivered under the caress of it, and nets along the shore were stretched like great webs to dry in the sublime warmth.

It was a reality and not a dream, and Carol was part of it.

CHAPTER FIVE

'THAT is settled.' His eyes came to her face and they held no expression of any sort to betray his inmost feelings. It was business with him, nothing more, and Carol thought how fearful and fascinating were the days ahead of her going to be. Yesterday she had been almost penniless with a growing boy to support, and now she was the betrothed of a rich man. It was a settled fact, he had just said so. A marriage that would be convenient for both of them.

'Come, let us go and find Terence,' he said, 'for he must be told the news by us before anyone else has the chance to fill his head with the wrong ideas.'

'Bedelia?' she asked, and even to say the name was to feel again a primitive recoil from the woman, as from a snake gliding out of the shadows into the sunlight. 'I'll tear the hair from her scalp if she ever harms my Teri!'

Rudolph paused and his eyes were like golden knives flicking across Carol's features. 'How passionately you care for him . . . as fierce as a Sabine in defence of your own. That was why the Roman soldiers stole the Sabine women, because they were wild and loyal and untouched by the decadence of soft living. You chose a good name for your son – the child takes after you for spirit, eh?'

Carol's heart turned over and she felt a clutch of fear, like a fist closing on her throat. What would he do if he discovered that he had a liar for a wife, and that he need never have married her, for Teri was not hers?

They walked along the wide *terrazza* in the direction of the lemon house, where he opened the door and called for Flavia. But the place echoed to his voice and the essence of citrus came out in a wave, engulfing Carol in its spiciness. They walked down steps into the heart of the garden that was rampant with oleanders, white petunias and scarlet geraniums. Scented clusters of camphor hung in the hot sunlight, and on the lower gradients there were tangled masses of Tuscan roses, and lilies like the trumpets of angels blowing a silent music. Santolina spilled from tall stone vases leading into cypress lanes, the thick silvery branches looped and braided together into intricate patterns.

They entered a stone-walled patio where niches in the wall held the weathered statues of gods and goddesses. Here there was a sunken pool surrounded by a balustrade, and they found Flavia sitting on the steps reading a book while Teri leaned over the water and tickled the darting fish with his fingers.

Rudolph paused and caught Carol by the arm, holding her still as they watched the girl and boy who were his children by proxy. 'She's a pretty creature, don't you think?' he murmured, his eyes upon Flavia, her dark hair gleaming in the sunlight. 'She wishes me to allow her to become a Sister of Mercy, and I confess to you that I don't wish her to choose a life of unrelenting service to others. Yet if I refuse her I shall feel a brute. It's a dilemma I am finding hard to resolve. She's such a gentle creature and the life of a nun can be so demanding. What should I do, Carol?'

It was the first time he had spoken her name and her eyes widened with surprise, for her name sounded so unusual when he spoke it. She was also astounded that he should ask her advice, and yet why should she be? He was a man, and it would strike him as astonishing that a pretty young thing like his adopted daughter should wish to join a nunnery instead of having the romantic dreams that were more natural to a sixteen-year-old.

'Why not tell her, *signore*, that if she is still of the same mind when she is seventeen then you will bow to her wishes? She spoke to me at breakfast about her sense of being called to the life of a nun, and if this is still strong in her when she reaches her next birthday, then it would probably be cruel of you to dissuade her. After all, *signore*, you don't yourself regard marriage as heaven, do you?'

Again his eyes were penetrating hers with their golden steel, unwarmed by any personal feeling for her. They were like scimitars cutting down at her, so that she felt an instinctive need to back away from him. How on earth was she ever going to treat this man as a husband? How was it possible to react normally to him, in so many ways a scarred and unpredictable stranger?

'Do you regard marriage to me as a possible hell?' he asked. 'You may say so if you think so. I shan't be offended by your candour.'

'I think marriage to you will be like a duel,' she replied. 'Like a rapier you flick at a woman at unexpected moments, and it doesn't worry you that you leave a sting.'

115

'Only a sting?' he drawled. 'You can take that, can't you?'

'Up to a point,' she said. 'I have feelings and a temper, *signore*. I won't be tormented without hitting back.'

'Oh, women can hit back,' he agreed, an acid note of meaning in his voice. 'They aren't the helpless and charming angels they pretend to be, and as I said even Flavia will succeed in making me feel a brute if I oppose her. But I will do as you say, for I'm going to grant you a certain amount of common sense, my *fidanzata*, on account of that boy down by the pool. You have not made a mama's darling of him, yet I can sense the strength of the bond between you. Look, he has seen you!'

'Cally!' Teri jumped to his feet and came dashing up the steps to where Carol stood. 'Look at all those stone statues, and the fish are so tame they let you touch them. It is a real palace, and Flavia says I'm the little frog who will turn into a prince.'

'Are you, Buster?' She brushed his hair out of his wondering eyes. 'You think you'll be happy here?'

'If you're staying as well,' he nodded, and he cast a look at the tall figure of the *baróne* as if to let him know that he wouldn't dream of staying anywhere without his Cally.

'You will both live here from now on,' Rudolph told him. 'Your mother and I are going to be married – do you know what that means, *caro*?'

Teri pushed the tip of his tongue against his upper lip and gave the question his consideration. 'Do you mean you're going to be my *papà* as well as Flavia's?' he asked.

The *baróne* inclined his head, but this didn't seem to please Teri. He edged close to Carol and caught her by the hand. He pushed his head against her and whispered something.

'What did he say?' Rudolph raised an eyebrow at Carol, but his voice was perfectly level.

'He – he says you're not to touch me.' She flushed. 'I'm afraid it's a bit of a phobia with him – we've been so close, you understand.'

'Then reassure the child.' Now the deep voice was ironic. 'Tell him that the ugly man will not be laying a finger on his adored mother.'

'Please don't be offended,' she said. 'Teri is like this with all men.'

'Have there been so many?'

'Of course there haven't!' Her flush deepened. 'But you have to remember that Vincenzo was dead by the time Teri was born, and we lived in a house run by my aunts. It's natural if he's a little – jealous.'

'Jealous?' The *baróne* spoke the word as if it were infinitely amusing. Then he extended a hand and drew Teri away from Carol. 'Come, *caro*, it will not be so bad to have a papa, will it? I shall be pleased to have a son so I can teach you all about boats and engines and the lore of the fruit trees. A man likes to have a son, you know.'

Teri gazed up at the *baróne*, and it must have been in that moment that he felt the compulsion that was older than time, older than man. He went towards that tall figure, and Carol could feel herself pressing a hand against her throat, as if to stifle something, as the child held out a hand to his uncle with an infinitely trustful gesture of acceptance. The small hand was lost in the large one, and the *baróne* gave Carol a brief look before saying to Teri:

'Come, let me take you to see the miniature motor-boats that I design before they are turned into real ones for people to use. We have a tank in the workroom on which we try them out, my assistant and I. You will like Marco, for he has magic in his fingers.'

'Magic?' echoed Teri, and Carol watched them out of sight among the camphor and almond trees, and her heart seemed to beat in time with the pulsating cicadas in the scented shrubs. Bees hummed in the purple wistaria, and above her head hung the glimmering eggs of silk in the mulberry trees.

If she felt doubts about this marriage, then she must stifle them as she had that sob in her throat. She and Teri needed a home where they'd be secure ... and that man was desperately lonely, though he would never admit it.

Teri could fill up some of the spaces in his heart ... those that a man reserved for a woman he was determined to keep empty and silent. No other woman was going to hurt him if he could prevent it.

Carol gazed down into the water of the pool, where the red-gold fish glimmered among the heart-shaped leaves of the floating lotus. It would be a strange marriage, that of two people disenchanted, who had both given their love to the wrong ones. No romance, no breathless desire to be close to each other, just two people drawn together by the needs of one small boy.

Flavia glanced up as Carol's shadow fell across the pages of her book. She smiled in her quiet way. 'It is good that the little one has made friends with Papà,' she said. 'Children are sometimes made afraid by the scars, you see.'

'Teri is no faintheart.' Carol sat down on the sun-warmed steps beside the girl who would soon be her stepdaughter. 'I have something to tell you – I hope you won't be shocked.'

'You look pale,' Flavia said. 'Is it something distressing?'

'It could be, for other people.' Carol took a deep breath. 'The *baróne* has asked me to marry him for the sake of – of giving Teri a legal name, and I have agreed to his proposal. I hope you won't mind?'

There was a bated silence, during which Flavia closed her book and held it gripped between her hands. 'So soon?' she murmured. 'You only came yesterday, and you must know what people will say.'

'Yes, I think I know what people will call me. It won't be true, Flavia. I'm not out for what I can get for myself, but I can't resist the security that such a marriage will provide for Teri. As he grows up he will be more aware of being fatherless, but if I marry the *baróne* then he won't have to be known as the love-child of Vincenzo Falcone. By the time he reaches his teens he will be fully accepted as the son of Rudolph, and I can't resist being a partner to that. After all, the *baróne* says that he will never marry otherwise, and he wants an heir for Falconetti. It's an ideal solution to my problem, and his. Don't you see that?'

'I see a marriage made without love,' Flavia replied. 'Could you endure that, Carol? You strike me as being a warm-hearted person, and you are English and not brought up to the arranged marriage.'

'No,' Carol agreed, 'but you have to realize that I haven't had stars in my eyes for a long time. Like Rudolph, I would only marry for Teri's sake, and if between us we can make the boy happy, then I think it will work out. The *baróne* is a man of honour. He wished to put his house in order.'

Flavia reached up to enfold a magnolia blossom in the palm of her hand. 'There are others of his house who won't be pleased. You know that, Carol?'

'Yes, I know.'

'I think Bedelia has hoped for a long time that Papà would make her the mistress of Falconetti, and if you marry him then she will hate you and find ways to hurt you.'

'Then I shall suggest that the *baróne* provide her with her own house. I shall have that right—'

'He won't turn her out if she wishes to remain here, Carol. Family feeling among Italians is very strong, and she is the widow of his dead brother.'

'But if she causes trouble I shall surely have the right to say she isn't welcome here.' Carol bit her lip and thought of the dark, autocratic face of her future husband. Would she have all that many rights as the wife of such a man? He didn't love her and was only marrying her because he thought her the mother of his brother's child. Beyond that link she meant absolutely nothing to him, whereas Bedelia was Italian and her union with Vincenzo had been the legal one.

A cold little chill ran through Carol even as the sun stroked her skin. She was the outsider here, the doors of Falconetti opened to her by the small hands of a child born of her sister Cynara.

'Oh, don't let me make you afraid.' Flavia looked suddenly contrite. 'It's wonderful that you love your little boy so very much, and I know that Papà can be kind. I am sure he will be kind to you.'

'Will he?' Carol looked about her at the serenity of the sunlit gardens, rising up into the blue-green cloisters of the eucalyptus trees. She saw the beauty and yet she felt strangely bleak ... did she want to be treated to a paternal kindness from the man who was going to be her husband? Was she never to know what it felt like to be loved?

'Anyway,' she forced a smile, 'you will wish us luck, won't you, Flavia? We're going to need it, aren't we?'

'I wish with all my heart that Papà could be a happy man,' the girl said softly. 'But it will always be hard for him to believe that a pretty woman could look at him and not be put off by his scars, and you are such a woman, Carol.'

'You think me so weak-kneed – oh, that isn't kind!' Carol exclaimed. 'I'm not that sort of person at all—'

'No, I mean that you are pretty and any man would like to take you to theatres and restaurants wearing nice clothes, but Papà stays here on the island where the people are used to him and don't hurt him by staring at his face and whispering about him. It will not be easy for you, being his wife, especially as you don't love him. Love can make all the difference, for then we see people with our hearts instead of our eyes.'

'That's true, and you, Flavia, are too wise and serious for your age.' Carol caught hold of the girl's hand and pulled her to her feet. 'Come with me and let us hunt about in the *palazzo* attics for some lighter furniture for Teri's bedroom. What he has at the moment is dark and a trifle grim and last night he was afraid to sleep alone. I daren't make a softie of him, not now he's going to be the son of the *signor baróne*.'

They entered the house and Flavia sought out the housekeeper and said they would be requiring footmen to help with the furniture, then they made their way to the attics, arriving breathlessly at the very top of the house, to spend the next couple of hours sorting out the accumulation of furniture discarded by the various *padrinas* but never quite disposed of, for much of it was quite valuable, reminding Carol of what Rudolph had said about the 'loot' of his ancestors.

They discovered an almost complete suite of Florentine bedroom furniture, much more graceful than the one which for Teri harboured goblins. It was installed by the good-natured footmen, and right away the room took on a lighter aspect. The great heavy drapes were taken down and replaced by nets with embroidered hems, and toys from the playroom were brought in, along with the Neptune chair and the clown.

'There!' Carol stood back to admire their handiwork. 'Isn't that much nicer for a child? Now when he looks about him he'll see those flowered murals instead of fearsome carvings. I wonder who the clown belonged to? It has quite a winsome face, don't you think?'

Carol picked up the clown, and then gave a sharp exclamation as something drove its point into her hand. She dropped the clown, which fell in a lop-sided cluster of limbs to the floor, and she stood there staring at the great drop of blood which something inside the toy had drawn from her hand.

'Don't touch it,' she warned Flavia. 'Someone has stuck a needle in it, or a long pin. It could have hurt Teri—'

Carol stood there sucking the palm of her hand, and into her eyes came an enraged look. Bedelia, she thought. Her idea of a sick joke.

'You had better put some iodine on your hand,' said Flavia, staring down at the clown, sprawled there on the carpet with a foolish look on its face. 'Who would do such a thing? Oh, surely it couldn't be deliberate – perhaps the clown needed mending and the needle or pin was forgotten and left in him by accident.'

'Perhaps.' The sting was going out of Carol's hand, but the suspicion remained in her mind. Gingerly she picked up the clown and carried him over to the window and carefully studied the back and front of him in the sunlight. Something glinted close against the padded body, the tip of a darning needle driven through the padding to emerge at the side of the toy, where a child would clutch it.

'Bitch!' Carol muttered to herself. Then she

marched out on to the gallery where one of the footmen was brushing the knees of his trousers. She asked him to fetch her a pair of pliers, and she stood there at the wrought-iron balustrade looking down on the *piano nobile* of the lower gallery. A woman was there putting flowers into a vase, white blossoms with dark leaves that she caressed with her pale slim hands.

Flavia came to the balustrade, and after a moment she murmured in Carol's ear: '*Il fiore della morte* – the flower of lovers whom death sets apart.'

'She hates me,' Carol said quietly. 'She's out to harm Teri.'

'Wash your hand in some iodine,' Flavia urged, but Carol waited until the footman came with the pliers and after she had drawn out the needle, which was over two inches long, she went down the stairs to Bedelia and held it out to her.

'You see this,' she said clearly, so that her voice carried around the hall, 'it's nasty and long and it hurts, and the next time you play one of your spiteful tricks on Teri I shall take this and jab it in you, up to the hilt, and I'm not making a threat but a promise.'

Bedelia gave her a haughty look. 'You're out of your mind, I should think. I never use sewing needles, for there are maids here to do that sort of thing, but I suppose where you come from you do all the menial tasks yourself. Really, I wouldn't know one end of a darning needle from the other.'

'Who said it was a darning needle?' Carol asked. 'It could be an embroidery needle, but you know all right that it has a big eye so wool can be threaded through it.

124

You're a jealous cat, but if you want to try your claws, then try them on me and not on a defenceless child. I can fight back and I will, *signora*.'

'I don't doubt it,' Bedelia sneered. 'I expect you have all the backstreet habits of your class – brawling, making threats, and selling yourself to a man no other woman would want!'

'That does it!' A quiver of sheer fury ran through Carol and taking hold of the flowers which Bedelia had just arranged she flung them in the woman's face, the soaking wet stems spattering the dark silk dress and falling around her in a mess of broken petals.

'What a delightful scene!' Curt as a whip the male voice cut across Bedelia's wailing. 'A man might think himself on the fish quay at Naples – be quiet, the pair of you! I have heard enough to know that you're equally at fault, two lovesick females fighting over a man who can make love to neither of you any more. Face it, both of you, and for heaven's sake behave with a little more dignity in my house.'

Carol stood there staring a moment at Rudolph, his face a dark mask of disgust and anger. Then she spun around and went running up the stairs, pursued by Teri, who didn't really understand and thought it all a bit of a lark.

'It was ever so funny,' he told Flavia, his dark eyes dancing with glee, 'but Zio Rudi got awfully angry and his eyes looked just like flames. He can be very fierce, can't he?'

'Yes, he can, *caro*.' Flavia gave Carol a concerned look. 'Are you all right—'

'She's trying to drive us away.' Carol felt as if she were shivering inwardly. 'He knows she's the one in the wrong, but did you hear what he said? It's so unfair, and for two pins I'd leave this place today and to the devil with marrying his excellency the *baróne*. Believe me, life was never a bed of roses, but it was never this thorny!'

For the remainder of the day Carol was in a restless, nervy mood, half torn between taking Teri away with her, and staying out of sheer obstinate refusal to be driven away by a woman's hatred and a man's total coldness of heart where she was concerned.

He had no feeling for her, and yet she had said that she would marry him. It was a kind of madness, only to be escaped if she packed their bags and hurried Teri away from the place.

He had his supper and she put him to bed in his own room, which he accepted now that the gothic furniture had been replaced, and the heavy-framed pictures taken down from the walls. She read him a story from *The Golden Wooden Shoes*, and very soon he was fast asleep. She studied him, indecisive about the future, and went into her own room to dress for dinner. The *baróne* would be good to the boy, she didn't doubt that for one moment, but she was just a disagreeable adjunct to the procedure of acquiring Teri for his son, and Carol could see no happiness for herself in becoming the wife of Rudolph Falcone.

None!

She bathed and dressed in a long dinner skirt of dark-honey velvet, with a champagne-coloured satin top, finished off by a gothic cross set with amethyst stones. Her hair was looped and folded at the nape of her neck, an intricate blonde knot against the pale slimness of her neck. She decided that she looked too pale and pensive and applied a dash of ruby colouring to her lips.

The mirror gave back her reflection and she saw an elegance and a composure that were only the outward semblance of a woman whose inner feelings were uncertain and stormy.

The *palazzo* felt very quiet as she made her way downstairs, pausing on her way to look at the faces in the paintings hanging on the walls; the eyes were smouldering, the features dramatic, and there seemed to be a glimpse of devil or tyrant, or wild Lothario riding off with another man's woman across the saddle-bow of a fast horse.

Lost in her reflections, one hand gripping the long skirt of her dress, Carol found herself entering the *salotto grànde,* where she gave a start upon finding Rudolph over by the long windows, framed by the scarlet folds of the floor-length window drapes. He wore a faultlessly tailored dinner-suit and white silk shirt, his shoulders taut and strong against the combination of fine materials.

'Good evening,' he said. 'What a change to meet a punctual woman! Will you take a glass of sherry, or perhaps you prefer a cocktail?'

'A – a sherry would be fine, *signore*.'

She watched him as he walked with supple silence across the carpets to the finely carved sideboard, on which stood a silver tray and a group of Venetian decanters of beautiful crystal glassware. Being alone with him after that earlier scene made her feel awkward, and she tried to find some ease of manner by looking around the fine old room, with its richly decorative ceiling and its Venetian chandeliers, a mass of cascading crystals on golden chains.

Silently he came across to her with the two fluted glasses of topaz wine, and she accepted hers with a husky murmur of thanks.

'To your health,' he said, and drank a little of his wine. Above the rim of his glass his eyes were upon her face, and there were tiny mocking lights in them, as if he too was remembering their last encounter in all its fishwife details.

'I – I can't marry you, *signore*.' The words burst from her lips, for they had been stored up in her throat all that afternoon, giving her an oddly choked-up feeling. 'It's out of the question and we both know it. Teri and I will stay here, if you want that, but I can't face being your wife.'

'That is too bad, but it doesn't change anything, and in your heart you know it. You have lived and worked for that boy and you won't take from him what I can give out of sheer pique because I wouldn't take your part against Bedelia. Look at me, Carol. Admit it!'

'You're so very sure of yourself, aren't you?' She gave him a resentful look. 'You have money, power, the will to please yourself, and you hold out a bone that I'd love to throw back at you. Oh, do you think I'd put up with any of you if it wasn't for Teri?'

'Do you think I'd ask you to marry me it it weren't for him?' The *baróne*'s voice was smooth and cold as steel. 'There will be no more indecision on your part, for I've already been in touch with my lawyers about drawing up settlement papers with regard to Terence. And I have also been looking at some of the family jewellery in order to find a suitable ring for my *fidanzata*.'

As he spoke he set aside his wine glass and came deliberately to where Carol stood. He took firm hold of her left hand and as if mesmerized she watched him slide on to her third finger a hoop of blood-red gems that caught the light of the chandeliers and burned with the kind of lustre that only came from genuine stones.

'How cold your hand is,' he said, and studied the ring against her skin. 'But the rubies look warm and they match your lips.'

Her heart thundered as his eyes found her mouth. His lips took on a quirk of irony. 'I'm not going to kiss you, if that's what you're afraid of, madam.'

'I – I'm not afraid,' she denied. 'But you seem to imagine that your face protects you from such a human thing as a kiss.'

'So you think me inhuman?' His eyes glittered down at her. 'Have you the courage to prove that I am?'

'Are you throwing out a challenge, *signore*?' She defied his eyes, but secretly felt as if the ground was quaking under her feet.

'Yes, madam, that is exactly what I am doing.' They were immediately under the chandeliers and the sparkling light was infinitely cruel upon his face, lean, high-boned, yet still distinctive despite the vicious acid burns. Carol felt each separate beat of her heart, and then impulse mastered her, and throwing an arm about his neck she reached up and pressed her lips against his disfigurement. She felt him go tense, and then too late she made a movement away from him. His arms closed around her like a vice and she was pulled almost brutally close to him and a startled cry opened her lips as he took them.

For five years Carol had lived like a nun, and now suddenly she felt the hard, smoky warmth of a man's mouth on hers. She felt her body crushed close to masculine muscles and impulses, and her every nerve was aware that it was hopeless to struggle. Her hand felt the smoothness of his nape and the peak of black hair cresting her fingertips. She felt the incredible hunger of his mouth, deep, deeper, until she was swept by a high wave of sheer feeling . . . feeling so warm and sensuous that she closed her eyes in order to savour what was happening to her.

Her eyes were still closed when he pushed her harshly away from him, and when her lashes blinked open he was standing there, looking at her as if he hated her.

'You see,' he said. 'In order to endure me, a woman has to do it with her eyes shut, not open, so she can blot out my face. Do you think I enjoy it, knowing that the woman in my arms is fighting not to push me away from her? Keep your kisses, madam! Keep your pity!'

'Oh, don't!' Carol flung up a hand, as if to ward off his tortured anger. 'You don't know what you're saying—'

'You think not?' He gave a cynical laugh and strode to the sideboard, where he replenished his wine glass. 'Your lip rouge is smudged, and I would prefer that we be looked upon as the usual sedate couple going through the first stages of a Latin courtship. If you were an Italian girl, I should have kissed your hand and nothing more.'

Carol, her knees tremulous, turned aside from him and taking her face-compact from her bag she looked at her lips in the tiny circular mirror. Her hand shook slightly as she wiped away the smudge which his lips had caused . . . his lips, hard, warm and so incredibly sensuous that the memory brought a wave of heat to her body. Oh God, what had got into her? Was she so love-starved that she actually wanted a man who had been hurt too deeply to ever feel anything more than a physical urge for a woman?

'It certainly won't worry me to have everything on a formal footing,' she said, and she drank her wine with as much composure as she could muster after that shattering experience in his arms. He certainly wasn't the statue he made out to be, and she hoped to heaven he hadn't realized the real truth . . . that his kisses had gone to her head with more potency than the wine. At eighteen, in the arms of Vincenzo, she had not felt this disturbed.

She lowered her eyes and felt the sting of a blush in her cheeks. How devastating Rudolph must have been when his looks had been unmarred and he had felt sure of his physical power over women. Even Vincenzo paled to a callow boy by comparison, and it occurred to Carol that she might have been completely bowled over by the *baróne* had she known him before another woman had ruined his face and made an embittered man of him.

'Now you do look suitably demure,' he drawled. 'What do you think of your ring? Does it feel as if it fits you all right?'

She looked down at the ring and was fascinated by the dense beauty of the gems. 'I've always liked the look of rubies,' she said. 'These are real, aren't they?'

'Of course they are. It's an old-old-fashioned ring, but I felt that you were not an ultra-modern young woman, not from the way you wear your hair and the way you dress.'

'I hope you don't think me a frump,' she protested, and glanced down at her long velvet skirt in some alarm. 'I – I haven't a large stock of dresses, but I hope that what I have is reasonably smart.'

'Perfectly charming,' he said, running his eyes up and down her figure. 'You dress to suit your style, and that is the essence of being soignée, is it not? I find short skirts and frizzy hair far from attractive, and you can rest assured, madam, that I find your appearance quite in keeping with the position of being my wife. Your stock of clothes will be enlarged, of course, and I am sure Gena will enjoy going with you to Rome to the dress houses.'

'Oh, but that isn't necessary,' Carol protested. 'I don't need any new things—'

'Perhaps not, but a trousseau is the accepted thing,

and you might as well enjoy what you can of our marriage.'

'You make it sound a very cold-blooded arrangement, *signore*.' Carol studied the ruby ring and thought to herself that such lovely, glimmering gems should belong to a love match. 'Have you quite given up hope of finding some sort of happiness?'

'What makes you think that I'm unhappy?' He raised an eyebrow as he looked at her, his eyes sheer amber and quite impenetrable. 'There is more to life, madam, than the idolatry of love between a man and a woman, if you are referring to that kind of happiness. No doubt you are.'

'I suppose so,' she admitted. 'Do you intend to hate all women because you were unfortunate enough to be hurt by one woman?'

'Hurt?' He raised a hand to his cheek, almost as if he felt the pain again and was shielding himself. 'As I told your son, a person recovers from physical pain, but there is another sort.'

'I – I realize that, *signore*. I gave my love to Vincenzo and he maltreated it, and it's hard to forget and forgive.'

'Then we are two people with something in common, eh?' His lips twisted into a smile that was quite cynical. 'We both find it hard to forget what has happened to us in the past, and because of that we are safeguarded from making fools of ourselves in future. At least married to me you won't be on your own and likely to attract another Lothario whose promises are like piecrust. There is substance to what I offer you even if there isn't any glamour.'

'Oh, I wouldn't say that, *signore*.' Carol glanced around the *salotto* with its beautifully carved furniture, its voluptuous Tiepolo ceiling, rich tapestry chairs and sofas, and these wine glasses with coiled serpent tails supporting the flared bowls. 'You have no idea how glamorous your house is by comparison to the cramped quarters Teri and I are accustomed to living in. You're used to living in a *palazzo*, but I find it altogether stunning . . . out of this world.'

'Yes,' he agreed, looking around him, 'I do probably take it for granted, and it will be good for the place that someone can appreciate its quaint attractions. It is very old and often the plumbing makes noises and goes wrong, the servants complain about the stairs and the size of the rooms and keeping the furniture well polished. The *palazzo* needs a mistress to care about it, so now you have a purpose and need feel no compunction that our relationship will not be intimate. You'll be free to enjoy the house without any need to entertain the master.'

'You enjoy being sardonic and scornful, don't you, *signore*? So your *palazzo* is to be my playhouse and the things in it my playthings, and like a child I'm to amuse myself and keep out of your way.' Carol gave him a candid look, a flicker of temper in her violet-grey eyes. 'If that is what you want, then it's all right by me. I'm not in the habit of imposing myself on anyone and I promise to keep my distance.'

'Good. We understand each other, don't we?' As he spoke he turned to face the door an instant before it opened to admit Gena and a man who looked to be in his middle thirties, clad rather more informally than the *baróne,* with a long-eyed, bony face, and cropped hair of a dusky red colour. When his eyes found Carol they were as green as a cat's, and they took her in from head to foot with the rapidity of the expert flirt, the pupils sharpening and intensifying his feline look.

'I'm thirsting for a Gimlet,' said Gena. 'May Saul shake them? He has the knack.'

'Be my guest,' said the *baróne* sardonically. 'How is the work going, Mr. Stern? I hope our island isn't proving too much of a distraction?'

'It has its distractions, but I'm being tough with myself.' The American approached the sideboard and began to measure out gin and lime-juice into a silver shaker. As he moved it gently back and forth he again looked at Carol.

'Don't I rate an introduction to the British guest?' he drawled. 'Gena failed to tell me that she was the regulation cool blonde beauty from those fabled shores.'

When he said this Carol instinctively glanced at the *baróne* and she saw his nostrils contract. But in a level voice he made the introductions, and then he added, quite deliberately: 'You might as well know, Gena, and you also, Mr. Stern, that Carol is going to be my wife.'

There was a breathless sort of silence, broken by Gena. 'Are you kidding, Rudi?' she exclaimed. 'You hardly know each other!'

'What is there to know?' he asked. 'Beyond that Carol has a son who needs a father; a boy so much a Falcone that no one need look at him twice without realizing that he is one of us. The marriage will ensure that Terence gets his due from the Falcone estate.'

'That part of it is immaterial to me, Rudi.' Gena shrugged her shoulders, partly bare from the cut of her smart evening dress. 'But marriage is such a serious step – a binding one for an ultra-Latin guy like yourself. Carol is British and her upbringing has been very different from yours, Rudi. You've always known that when it came to marriage – let's face it, you are titled and rich.'

'Circumstances are not what they were,' he broke in, his voice a trifle curt. 'Carol and I understand each other. We know what we want.'

'Well, it's your funeral.' Gena was looking at Carol as she spoke. 'As long as you know what you're taking on.'

'I think I do.' Carol tried to speak in a normal voice, and to behave as if she took all this in her stride. Inwardly she was as nervous as a kitten plucked out of its warm bed of straw to stand shivering in the middle of a vast, bright room full of strangers. She wanted to run out with a cry of fright, but had to control the urge and set her lips in a brave smile.

'Thanks, honey.' Gena took her Gimlet from Saul Stern. 'I need this more than ever.' She took a deep swallow, her eyes upon her brother's unrevealing face. 'When do you actually take the plunge?' she asked.

'As soon as everything is settled.' He spoke with perfect naturalness and stood there with the chandelier full on his face. Carol could see the American writer staring at him with those cat-green eyes, and she could

136

almost read his mind. Everyone would assume the marriage to be a normal one, and she knew that Saul Stern, with his lean and lazy unscarred face, was wondering how a woman would feel in the arms of a man who had been hideously hurt by having vitriol flung at him.

They were standing like that, each of them testing the situation and its implications, when Bedelia entered the *salotto*. Tonight she had obviously set out to prove that the English girl couldn't hold a candle to her when it came to being seductive. She wore a classic dress of burgundy crushed-velvet and gold bracelets gleamed on her arms. Her eyelids were shadowed and she had the skin to be seen on Latin patios, pale and silky like the magnolia flowers growing there. Her silky hair was piled high on her head and secured by jewelled pins.

'Oh, am I the last down?' she asked, in a voice whose texture matched her skin and hair. 'How naughty of me to keep all of you waiting!'

'We're only having dinner,' Gena drawled. 'We aren't on our way to a ball.'

'Yet I took this for a special occasion,' Bedelia replied, and her eyes flicked across Carol's face. 'I thought I should dress up for such a momentous evening, for I had quite given up hope that dear Rudi would ever find himself a woman.'

'Damn you—' Gena raised her glass as if to throw its contents in Bedelia's face, but Saul caught her by the wrist.

'Don't waste good gin, Gena *mia*,' he grinned. 'Sticks and stones can't hurt your brother. He's what they call one of nature's gentlemen.'

'I know,' said Gena, giving her sister-in-law a murderous look. 'But I'm no lady.'

'No, dear.' Bedelia was quite unruffled as she played with one of her bracelets and smiled at her own thoughts. 'And you've no need to advertise your liberation, for we all know that you don't follow the Latin principle of a woman keeping her purity for the man she marries. I am sure the entire population of the *isola* is aware that you spend entire nights at the beach house – perhaps you do typing for Mr. Stern? If so, then I do apologize for my naughty thoughts.'

'You're about as naughty as a damned python,' Gena retorted. 'And you can mind your own business about what I do – in fact a few sessions of slap and tickle might make a human being of you. *Santo Dío,* no wonder Vince ran out on you! You and Vince! It was always good for a laugh!'

'That will be enough.' The *baróne*'s voice was controlled but as cutting as a rapier edge, honed fine and sharp on his personal suffering at the hands of a woman. 'This is, I hope, a civilized household and not the fish market where women hurl abuse at each other. All of you are here at my invitation, but my patience and so-called instincts of a gentleman are not so reliable as you might assume. Do I make myself clear?'

'As crystal, brother dear.' Gena went to him and took him by the arm with beguiling affection. 'If I were you I'd have thrown the lot of us out on our ears a long time ago. Because you're a cynic you are curiously tolerant, aren't you, Rudi? You know that people aren't angels, so you don't expect them to behave as if cowed down by their haloes. I think you are the man who has spoilt other men for me – and that includes you, Saul, honey.' She shot an impudent smile at the American. 'You should have known Rudi in his heyday. Now he hides himself away because he thinks women only go for pretty faces.'

'I don't hide away,' he growled. 'I prefer a quiet life to a rowdy one. The island suits me and I can work here without getting involved in the managerial side of things as in Rome. My imagination takes flight in my *falconiere*.'

'I envy you, *signore*,' said Saul, as they began to make their way into the dining-room, where an oval-shaped table was beautifully laid under another of those crystal-hung chandeliers, throwing its sparkling light down on to lace and fine old china, and pink Tuscan roses spilling from a silver centrepiece among feathery green ferns.

'Do you, Mr. Stern?' The *baróne* looked with absolute irony at the writer, who was so obviously a man who strolled through life, taking his pleasures as they came and not concerned what the next day might bring. Catlike he would charm and be friendly, and then stroll away without looking back. That was how Carol summed him up as she took her place at the table and opened a lace-edged napkin on to her knees.

'Why not?' Saul smiled so that his eyes narrowed to emerald slits in his lean face. 'It's every man's dream to have an island of his own, and yours has solitude and beauty without being miles from the civilized world.'

'I am gratified that you're enjoying your stay on the

isola.' There was a dry note in the deep Latin voice, and Carol saw the way Rudolph glanced at his sister, as if he knew all about her without having to learn the details from Bedelia. Yes, a cynic was more inclined to be tolerant than a man who had faith in his fellow creatures. Most people had a clay heel, and Rudolph would be painfully aware of it. Carol caught at her lip with her teeth as she recalled the way he had induced her to unbind her hair for him, yet he told her that intimacy was ruled out of their life together ... their married life.

Lost in her thoughts, she gave a start as a hand touched her wrist. 'Has Rudi given you a ring?' It was Gena reaching for her left hand and showing it off to the others at the table. The light shone in the rubies, exquisitely carved and gleaming with a deep lustre that was unbearably lovely.

'The tiger rubies!' Gena exclaimed. 'Rudi has started to give you those – a whole set, you fortunate girl, brought from India aeons ago by one of our ancestors. They always go to the bride of the *baróne*! Look, everyone, isn't it a perfectly beautiful ring?'

Carol felt the stare of dark eyes and when she glanced up she found Bedelia looking at her with sheer hatred in her gaze. Her heart lurched and now she was quite certain that Bedelia had wanted the *baróne* and all the material things he could give a woman. Now Carol stood in her way ... Carol and Vincenzo's son.

'Have the rubies a story?' Saul asked. 'They sound as if they might have, and my writer's curiosity is aroused.'

'They belonged to an Indian prince,' said Gena, trailing a smile from her brother to Carol. 'This ancestor of ours was out there in this feudal region in the hills, on a tiger hunt, and one day he and the prince were riding together when one of the great cats leapt from a rock and would have brought down the lordly Indian if the sporting Italian had not been quick on the draw. He saved the prince's life and the rubies were given to him to be made up into jewellery for his bride when he took one – he was at that time a cynical bachelor like Rudi. He remarked that they glowed just like the tiger's eyes as it leapt to kill, and from then on they had that name attached to them. Thrilling enough for you, Saul? And for you, Carol?'

At once Carol was the centre of attention, and only too aware of what was going through the minds of those who looked at her, her blonde looks giving her an outwardly cool look, hiding the turmoil that was going on inside her.

'Come, let us forget the saga of the rubies and proceed with dinner,' said the *baróne*, coming to her rescue in a suave voice. She didn't dare to look at him and turned gratefully to the manservant in order to serve herself with vegetables; delicious *sauté* potatoes, broccoli spears, courgettes and carrots to accompany baked veal with gravy. She was a little too churned up to really taste the food, the proceedings a vortex of voices, the swing of golden earrings in Gena's ears, a subtle aroma of ambergris, and the gleam of silverware.

She was glad when they left the table to return to the *salotto*, where they drank coffee and a very old brandy in cut-glass bowls.

'Play for us, Rudi.' Gena was wandering about restlessly, her brandy bowl in her hand, a chain of tiny golden hearts glistening at her throat. 'I'd offer to sing, but I feel rusty after so many months away from the stage, and you were always better at everything than poor little me.'

Saul gave a laugh at that. 'Do you ever stop acting?' he asked her.

'Darling, if I ever stopped acting then I might start crying,' she rejoined, and as the light caught her face Carol wondered how much truth there might be in her words. Gena obviously adored her brother, and would have grown up thinking him a dashing dark knight. Had she not said that he had spoiled all other men for her?

Carol watched him as he walked in his supple way to the grand piano and sat down on the long padded bench in front of the keyboard. Gena touched a switch and immediately only the piano candles gave light to the room and deep shadow lay in pools, hiding the gold-brocaded chairs and their occupants.

Near where Carol sat the *salotto* windows were open and the night air that blew into the room was filled with the scent of syringa and nicotine-flower.

The strong, lean hands moved on the keys and the *Liebestraum* music filled the night with its nostalgia. Somehow it didn't surprise Carol that the *baróne* could play so well; music lay in the Italian soul, along with a certain strain of sadness that was very Latin. She felt moved, and she felt afraid. Was it possible that she was growing to care for the man . . . caring for someone was so dangerous, for it made you so vulnerable.

A shiver ran through her slender body; a combination of emotions ranging from apprehension to that of being deeply moved by the music. The pianist played on her feelings with the same firm touch with which he played the piano; sure of what he wanted and sweeping her along with him as he swept his strong, slim hands along the keyboard.

When the silence came she must have gasped aloud, for at once she caught the flash of his eyes, transfixing her own across the room, compelling her to do as he wished like some dark magician, with the power to make her go to him like a sleeper in a dream, until her hand was at rest upon his shoulder.

'You play like a master,' she said shyly. 'A man like you shouldn't be marrying a woman as ordinary as I am.'

'You sell yourself cheap, my dear,' he drawled, gazing up at her in the soft glow of the electric candles. 'We are Beauty and the Beast, as in the classic tale of magic . . . as it should be, perhaps, for two strangers who have come together in a strange way. Have you a favourite piece of music? I might know it.'

'I – I don't go in for modern music, if you were wondering, *signore*.' A smile quivered on her mouth. 'Didn't you call me an old-fashioned girl?'

'So I did.' His eyes swept over her glimmering halo of hair, and she no longer felt calm or shy but stormily aware of him as a man who had touched her hair, stroking those lean fingers down over the silky length of it. She drew away from him, afraid of feelings that were quite unrelated to what she had felt whenever she had been close to Vincenzo. There was a power to Rudolph that she had never felt in any other person; he had plumbed the depths of pain and she was awed by him and out of her depths when it came to dealing with him.

She glanced over her shoulder and saw that Gena and Saul had slipped away into the garden, and deep in a silken chair Bedelia was watching the two of them at the piano, the glitter of her eyes matching the gems on her hand as she raised her wine glass to her lips. Carol felt herself at the centre of storm currents whose full force she had yet to endure. It took courage to stand there and defy Vincenzo's widow, a woman who had waited years to secure the *baróne*, only to see him become engaged to an English girl he hardly knew.

'I'd hardly have thought it the trait of an old-fashioned girl to have a child by a married man,' Bedelia purred. 'Or were you such an innocent that my Vincenzo had only to look at you in order to make you his plaything? Terribly handsome, was he not? Women spoiled him, ruined him, and you were one of them for all your wide-eyed air of injured innocence. I hope you are grateful to Rudi for giving your child such a chance of a lifetime. You should kiss his boots, you little slut!'

The softly played music ceased abruptly and the silence had thunder in it. Then Rudolph towered to his feet and at once his face and its expression were shadowed.

'I will only say this once more to both of you,' he said

harshly. 'If and when you fight over the dead bones of Vincenzo, then do it away from my presence. No one pretends that Carol is marrying me for any reason but to give my brother's child a name – the reason is understood and accepted, but by the devil, I won't have my future wife and my sister-in-law at each other's throats in my house. The pair of you can get out if it persists, but I will keep the boy, and that isn't a threat but a promise!'

As he said this he slammed down the lid of the piano and gripping Carol by the elbow he marched her from the *salotto* and across the mosaic tiling of the hall to the stairs. She was forced to mount them until they arrived at the door of her suite, and there he paused and glowered down at her, his scars standing out with devilish clarity.

'Alive or dead, my brother still possesses the pair of you,' he gritted. 'But the boy I mean to have. I'll do my utmost to see that he isn't possessed by the devil!'

'You – you talk of devils,' Carol gasped, too shaken to choose her words. 'Look at you, *signore*! What do you think you are like in a temper – a saint?'

His brows blackened and he actually bared his teeth at her. 'I don't look at myself if I can avoid it, madam, but you will have to. It's the price you pay for making good that sin of yours.'

'My sin?' Her heart almost stopped beating, and then she felt the intolerable ache of having to hold back the truth. 'I – I was incredibly innocent – more than you'll ever know.'

'Doubtless.' He said it with great sarcasm. 'Always

the excuse after the deed—'

'He married me,' she gasped. 'I told you—'

'Then why,' the *baróne* lowered his voice and bent his head so that his face came closer to her, 'do you always look so guilty when we speak of Vincenzo? The acid burned my flesh, not my eyes, and I see that look on your face right now. The look of a guilty woman!'

'Oh – let me go!' Carol tried to tug her hand from his, but his fingers were steely and unsparing, holding her at his mercy. 'You – you enjoy tormenting people, don't you?'

'It's one of the few pleasures I have left.' His lips twisted into a smile. 'If I was ever gentle, then the acid made away with it as it destroyed half my face. Look well at me, Carol. This is the face you will be living with.'

She looked . . . Beauty and the Beast, he had said. The beast secure in his kingdom of fear, and not to be overcome until someone dared to be unafraid of him.

With sudden defiance Carol stopped pulling away from Rudolph and throwing her free arm about his neck she reached up and pressed her lips to his scars. They felt strange and unreal, and any sense of shock was held in abeyance until he suddenly caught his breath, then crushed her to him and kissed her mouth with a savagery that left it bruised and stung.

'Never play with fire,' he almost snarled against the side of her neck, his breath arching warm against her skin. 'Getting burned is never very pleasant, take it from me.'

He swung away from her and strode off along the

Italian gallery, watched by the painted eyes in the portaits along the panelled walls. He vanished, leaving a silence loud with the harsh mockery of his words ... his kisses.

Stifling a sob, Carol flung herself into her bedroom and slammed the door behind her.

CHAPTER SIX

IT seemed like ages, pressed there against the closed door, until Carol felt calm enough to go into Teri's room to ensure that he hadn't moved about in his sleep and pushed off his bedcovers. He lay in a small half-moon, fast asleep in the soft glow of the night-lamp, his long lashes dark on his cheeks. Carol bent to him and gazed intently at his dreaming face . . . yes, there it was again, that strange resemblance to Rudolph in the fine bone chiselling of the childish face. The man had seen it for himself, and he knew that as Teri grew older he would grow to resemble him more and more.

A son at second-hand for the *baróne* of the island, who had put love out of his life, living almost like a monk even though he kissed a woman with the savage passion of an experienced man.

Very gently Carol drew the covers around the boy, and then she returned to her own vast bedroom and stood there in a rather lost way. She gave a start when the clock chimed, and when she saw how late it had grown she began to prepare for bed.

She was in her robe, her long hair down about her hips, when the silence of her room was broken by a brief rapping sound on the door. She almost dropped the hairbrush, and there in the mirror she saw the look of alarm in her eyes. Her heart hammered. Oh God, was this Bedelia, defying the *baróne* in her bitterness, unable to stop making those venomous remarks that left their sting?

Carol stood there tensely, watching the door through the mirror and hopeful that whoever stood there would presume that she was in bed and go away again.

It wasn't to be! Abruptly the door swept open and a tall figure stood in the aperture, clad in a robe of some rich dark material. Carol stared at him, so suddenly nerveless that she couldn't have moved or spoken had she wanted to. She had to suffer his eyes upon her, raking over her face and down over her hair that glistened like a pale gold cape around her.

'It isn't good for people to part in anger,' he said, and his voice seemed extra deep in his throat. 'The morning may never come and then it's too late to ask forgiveness. May I come in?'

'Aren't you in, *signore*?' Carol forced a smile that felt as if it were pinned to her face – it hurt.

'It is better to close the door,' he said, 'in case someone should pass by and see me.'

'My reputation is already in shreds,' she rejoined. 'And you are the feudal lord of the *isola*, aren't you, with power over all of us who live on your land?'

'That is the romantic exaggeration of a woman.' As he closed the door his eyebrow quirked, and Carol saw from the look in his eyes that he was reading her mind. 'Have you yet seen me going around with a whip in my hand?'

'You don't need a whip, do you, *signore*? A look from you can be enough.'

'Oh, yes, quite enough to make anyone flinch,' he

agreed sardonically.

'I refer to your inherent power,' she said, her fingers clenching on the hairbrush as she remembered her own feeling of utter helplessness in his arms. It wasn't just physical strength that he possessed; a feeling of steel in the taut muscles and hard flesh of him. He had an iron control over himself, and it extended to other people. He wasn't a man who lived on his senses as Vincenzo had, but neither was he cold, without feeling. He was something of a tiger and he knew how far to let out the leash on himself.

Carol watched him and knew that shining threads of excitement were woven into her terror of this man. He had kissed her and now they were aware of each other as man and woman. They couldn't ignore the fact that his lips and body had left their mark on hers, and standing there facing him she still felt the bruises left by his savage grip on her.

'Are you afraid of me?' he asked, almost casually. 'The room doesn't seem cold, and yet I saw you shiver just then.'

'Let's say, *signore*, that I'm afraid of the position I find myself in.'

'A woman alone in her bedroom with a man, eh?' His eyes taunted her. 'One would think you still a virgin, untried in the ways of a man.'

'I'm referring to being married to you. You might expect me to be at your feet – like a peasant woman. Or trailing at your heels. As your sister implied, you are marrying out of your class.'

'I do as I please.' In a couple of long strides he was

across the room and darkly overpowering as he stood over Carol. 'The opinions of other people mean nothing to me, and I should hope I am not such a boor that I would expect you to humble yourself in any way at all. You will be the *padroncina*, way above the other women. *My wife.*'

The two words daggered through Carol. His wife because the solemn words made it so, along with the witnesses and the ring, and the fact that she took his name.

His wife . . . the stranger at the altar beside him.

'A woman expects romance, eh?' His voice was deeply ironic. 'Was there not enough of that with my brother?'

'More than enough,' she admitted. 'But when someone says they love you, then somehow it's easier to be married to them. It establishes a bond, but you and I – we grasp at nothing, because there is nothing between us. Don't you see?'

'Yes, I see.' He gazed down at her, and his eyes followed the silky flow of her hair. 'There is no sense of security without love, and I can only give you the material things. They will have to be enough, *mia*, for the sake of Vincenzo's son. Marriage to me will make him secure, at least.'

'Yes,' she murmured, and felt a dreadful aching at her heart. Had she foolishly hoped that Rudolph might speak of love instead of underlining the fact that he had only the comfort of his home to offer and never the consolation of his heart?

'I could never deny that I want Teri to be safe,' she

said. 'You must think me horribly ungrateful—'

'I merely think of you as a woman.' He shrugged his shoulders. 'You wouldn't be the first to give your heart to a knave, and to bury it in his grave. But you are young, and perhaps a life that is a little easier will help you to forget in time. It will be good here for the child, among his own sort of people, especially as you said that he was not made welcome in the house of your aunts.'

'They're a little old-fashioned, *signore*.' Carol looked at him with troubled eyes; he believed that she was smitten by an undying love for his brother, and she couldn't tell him that whatever she had felt for Vincenzo had been struck dead in her heart on the very day he had falsely married her. At the time she had hated him, but now she felt only a residue of regret and pity.

Here with Rudolph, in the solitude and quietness of this Italian bedroom, she felt strangely breathless and unlike herself. She looked at his seared face and wanted to offer him something . . . he was a man after all, and he had kissed her with a kind of banked-down hunger for passion.

'Won't you feel cheated' – the words stumbled from her lips – 'married to someone just for the sake of – of her child?'

'Cheated?' His eyes fixed hers with a dark brilliance. 'Are you saying that you want to give yourself to me, *signora*?'

'When we – marry.' The words almost fainted in her throat. 'If you want me—'

'Oh, I can want.' Swift as a striking snake his hand

flicked out and took a fistful of her hair, pale and gleaming against his dark skin. 'I assure you, madam, that it would give me the intensest pleasure to throw you to that bed and take your body. But pleasure is a passing thing and it bears no relation to the real joy – the joy that is love.'

His eyes held hers a moment longer, then with a brief inclination of his raven-dark head he turned on his heel and strode to the door. It opened and closed behind him, leaving a blank space where his dark shape had been. Carol stared at the emptiness and felt as if she had been slapped around the face.

She lifted a hand to her face and felt the coldness of her skin. He couldn't have said it more explicitly, that she was just a body that might please him for an hour. Beyond that she had nothing to offer him that he wanted . . . this shaken feeling was horrible, for it told her that her proffered heart had been flung back at her.

'Oh – go to hell,' she muttered, and tossing her long hair she made for her bed, climbed the half-moon of steps and crept in under the covers like a lost cat seeking a little warmth.

There in the darkness she thought over their conversation until her cheeks burned. The man was abominably arrogant and so withdrawn from all sympathy that trying to please him was like getting entangled in barbed wire. All right, if that was the way he wanted it then she'd be happy to oblige him by accepting the material advantages of being his wife. No one before had ever treated her as anything more than the dutiful standby who took on an abandoned baby and slaved for a pair of selfish aunts in order to keep a roof over that baby's head. She had earned a little respite from drudgery, and it would certainly make a change to be the *padroncina* who gave the orders instead of taking them.

Carol fell asleep on that thought and when she awoke in the morning that feeling of defiance was still with her. She met the bold eyes of the aristocratic officer in his carved picture frame and dropped him a curtsey. 'Yes, *signore*, you may look down your proud nose, but that doesn't alter the fact that I'm going to marry into your high and mighty family.'

Without delay or hindrance the *baróne* carried out his wedding plans, and there were certain papers which Carol had to sign in the presence of a rather starchy lawyer from Rome. When she asked Rudolph about the papers he replied that they related to Teri and legal preparations were being made for the boy to·take his name and to become heir to Falconetti.

Carol's heart came into her throat as she realized that she was committing another woman's child into the keeping of the *baróne*, and that in some awful way she might be breaking the law. But now there seemed no way to stop the momentum of the arrangements; she actively feared Rudolph's anger if he should discover that she had tricked him into accepting her as Teri's mother.

Gena carried her off to Rome for a shopping spree, and there in one of the biggest and smartest dress houses her clothes for the wedding and the honeymoon were fitted and purchased. Lovely things in real Eastern silks, and in dreamy colours that suited Carol and brought out a rather enchanting quality in her blonde looks.

'Now I know why Rudi is marrying you,' said Gena, walking around Carol after a sumptuous velvet dress had been tried on her slim figure, with slashed medieval sleeves and a low neckline which revealed her creamy neck and shoulders. 'My dear, you pay for dressing, as the saying goes, and have a certain look of class in good clothes. That hair of yours helps, of course, and now I can see why you never had it chopped off. Were you hoping to marry a rich guy one of these days?'

Gena smiled, but there was a certain glint of shrewdness in her eyes. Carol met that smile with a faintly mysterious look, of which she was totally unaware, for she wasn't looking at herself in the long mirror.

'I think you know I'm not a gold-digger,' she said. 'Chance plays strange tricks with our lives, that's all.'

'Perhaps.' Gena stood and studied the effect of Carol in the velvet dress the colour of sapphires. 'All the same, you've been damned lucky, haven't you, honey? Do you love my brother? He deserves it, but women are put off by his cool air of pride in the face of his deformity. He won't be pitied, if that's what you feel for him.'

'I know how much he hates sympathy,' Carol said. 'Anyway, I'm not the important feature of this marriage, and these clothes are only a little icing on the cake. Rudolph is marrying me for the sake of Teri.'

155

'And vice versa, eh?' Gena frowned, and then turned to consult with the fitter over some of the other fine items for Carol's wardrobe. The violet and fawn riding outfit, the gown embroidered with a filigree of garnets and gold thread, the textured suits and glove-leather shoes.

Carol played the obliging, shy bride and refused to allow the secret fears and feelings to overwhelm her. She lunched with Gena and Saul in smart restaurants, and was taken on a tour of the city. It all passed in a dreamlike fashion and she wasn't really sorry when it was time to return to the *isola*, where Teri had been left in the charge of the *baróne*'s kindly and efficient housekeeper.

All the time away from him Carol had been anxious in case Bedelia should harm him in any way . . . when he rushed into her arms in the hall and she hugged him breathless, her anxiety gave way to a glowing smile, which the *baróne* caught and held as he emerged from one of the archways. His eyes flashed over, taking in her clover-coloured suit, her legs long and slim in transparent silk stockings, the kind worn with a wispy suspender-belt. Carol was unbearably aware of him looking at her, clad like this in the expensive garments his money had bought, and which Gena had insisted that she wear now she was the bespoken of a wealthy Italian. She was aware that they heightened her fair looks and gave her an ultra-feminine appearance, somehow taking from her that air of independence she had felt in her inexpensive trouser suits bought in a chain store.

'Welcome home,' he said, coming across to her. 'Are you making sure that your *bambino* is still in one piece and has come to no harm during your absence?'

There was a curious note of indulgence in his deep foreign voice, and it disarmed Carol and made her legs tremble as she straightened up.

'Hullo, *signore*. I'm glad you've taken good care of Teri.'

'Quite naturally I have kept my eye upon him.' A lean hand reached out and briefly stroked across the boy's head. 'Teri and I are now friends, are we not, *mio*?'

'Zio Rudi has taken me fishing in his boat, Cally.' The boy smiled up eagerly at her, and she gave a little gasp of dismay as she saw that he had lost a front tooth.

'Buster, how did that happen?'

'On a walnut,' he said. 'We found some in the orchard, but Zio said it was only a baby tooth and that from now on I would start to grow my real teeth.'

She glanced at Rudolph and he broke into a slight smile, showing his own faultless white teeth. Teri would have teeth like that, she thought, thankfully. Strong, hard and white. Teri would be safe now, to grow up in this man's protection.

Her smile was shaky. 'I – I brought you back a present, Buster. Shall we go upstairs and unpack it?'

'Oh, yes, come on!' He tugged at her hand, and all the way up the stairs she could feel the *baróne*'s eyes upon them. She felt again that tremor in her legs; a hasty glance revealed that the *baróne* was still at the foot of the staircase and his eyes were upon her legs as she mounted to the gallery. The pulse gave a skip at the base of her throat and she recalled in all its detail that night in her bedroom and the almost ruthless way he had said that it would give him intense pleasure to 'take' her.

She swayed slightly and caught at the wrought-iron handrail of the stairs ... It was crazily foolish and wanton, but she wanted the reality of that threat, with or without any love in it. Pity? She felt not a scrap of it for such a man, her female instincts far more aware of his strength and lean hard grace in the cream-coloured jacket and silk-striped brown shirt that set off his intense darkness. His smile curled against his acid-hurt, ironic lips that had left their lingering impression upon hers.

'Why are you shivering like that, Cally?'

Teri's young voice fluted the words up and down the stairs, and instantly she saw the smile wiped from the scarred face, the pupils narrowing in those tawny eyes. He turned and walked away in the direction of his den, taking with him the belief that she was repulsed by the look of him.

Her fingers so gripped the iron that her bones ached. She wanted to dash down the stairs to Rudolph, with such an overwhelming urgency that she barely controlled the impulse. What was the use? If she touched him, if she met his eyes, she would only be struck dumb by shyness and it would only look as if she were trying to say sorry to him.

'I can't wait to see what you've bought me.' Teri was tugging at her other hand, and that moment of urgency was safely disposed of. Getting emotionally involved with the *baróne* could only lead to further complications, and she had enough of those to handle without losing her head over a man because he had something about him that appealed to the primitive side of her nature . . . the side she hadn't been aware of until meeting him, living in a kind of innocence that now made her understand Cynara a little better.

Desire could blind you to everything else, and now she was aware of its danger Carol resolved to be on her guard with the man who aroused it. It had nothing to do with love . . . love was a tender emotion, not a savage urge to give and take.

Only a matter of days now separated Carol from her marriage to the *baróne*, and she filled them with as much activity as possible, seeking in every way not to be alone with the man who was to be her husband.

The morning of the wedding dawned with brilliant sunlight, and the first thing Carol heard when she awoke was the sound of the bells in the Falconetti chapel, pealing among the trees with that very special sound that even a bride of expediency couldn't help but respond to. She ran out on to her balcony and stood there barefooted in her pyjamas, her hair in its long thick plait making her look very young and vulnerable.

'*Buon giorno!*' The words floated up to her from the courtyard, and when she glanced downwards there was the *baróne* on horseback, saluting her with a flick of his whip. He held it as if reminding her of what she had said, that he had power over people without the use of a whip.

'Good morning, *signore*,' she called down to him, and a potent shyness clutched at her throat as her fingers clutched at the lapels of her pyjama jacket, pulling them together over her bare neck. A black sweater was high against his throat, and his boots and breeches gave him a tough look. His black hair was ruffled as if he had been riding hard, and this was verified by the way his horse tossed its head and stamped the cobbles.

'I – I don't think I'm supposed to see you before the – ceremony,' Carol said, and she was about to back into her room when he commanded her to stay where she was.

'I thought only we Latins were superstitious,' he said. 'You look rather pale and nervous, as if this were the first time you had gone through with this kind of thing. I should be the nervous one, eh?'

'You!' she exclaimed. 'I can't imagine you, *signore*, being nervous of anything, least of all a mere girl.'

'Yes, how very young you look, Carol, as you must have looked on the morning you went to church with my brother. Then it was *sposalizio della vergine*, was it not?'

'Yes,' she said faintly, for that was the only truth about her marriage to Vincenzo. She had been very young and unawakened, and because of an inner loneliness so prepared to share her heart with a good-looking charmer whose irresponsibility had revealed itself even before her wedding day was over. Added to the pain of that memory was the knowledge that he had been a bigamist, with a wife in Italy, and she felt that it was rather cruel of Rudolph to remind her of that far-off morning when she had faced a happy day which had ended in tears in her single bed.

He wasn't to know that, of course. He thought her a woman who had experienced lovemaking, and pregnancy, and the bringing into the world of a baby boy.

That band of terror seemed to lock itself around Carol's throat and she stood there in the full sunlight, looking petrified.

'Oh, there's no need for such a display of bridal jitters,' he said, jeeringly. 'You and I know our wedding score, don't we?'

'Please—' But the words wouldn't come, locked in her throat by the twin keys of her fear of him. A man who was being tricked into marriage, unaware that Teri had been abandoned by his real mother. A man who disturbed Carol in such a physical way that some nights she lay sleepless and restless, as if the thick mattress of her bed was stuffed with pins.

'It's too late for either of us to back out,' he told her, almost harshly. 'The people of my island are all set for a celebration, and you have signed documents that already make me the father of your son. *Che sarà, sarà!*'

'What will be, will be,' she echoed, and she stood there with her hands gripping the parapet rail, feeling as if she were about to launch herself into the unknown, with a man who in every way was still unknown to her.

'*Bella donna,*' he mocked, 'please, in church don't look as if I plan to beat you each day. The people of the *isola* are expecting a radiant bride who has made a

161

good marriage – at least try and look as if you're en-amoured of my money even if you feel cold shivers instead of warm thrills when you look at me.'

Already emotionally torn in two as she was, his words shattered her and the tears filled her eyes and hung there glistening before breaking on her cheeks.

'I – I shall marry you without any illusions, shan't I?' She spoke stormily and wished she could hate him; if she hated him it would somehow be easier to marry him, for it wouldn't matter that she had lied to him and signed her name to a false declaration that Teri was her son.

Her sister Cynara had only to change her mind about wanting Teri and the atmosphere would be filled with the blistering heat of the *baróne*'s anger. Carol shrank visibly from what she envisioned, and his sharp eyes saw and taunted her for that shrinking motion.

'Now you can run away, but no further than your bedroom. Later you will have to put on a brave and lovely face, my bride – I insist on it. Anyway, I shall be sending you something which should assist you in making a quick recovery from your loss of composure. For now, *arrivederci*.'

With a motion of his riding whip he cantered off towards the stables, a line of white-painted doors beyond an archway draped in morning glory. Carol listened until the hoofbeats died away, but still there was a soft drumming and it came from her heart. Her foolish heart had led her into this, and there was no going back to the dreary normality of life at Chalk-leigh. She could only hope and pray that the Aunts, having been told that she was to marry the *baróne*, wouldn't contact Cynara in America and wake some latent maternal instinct in her sister ... the bells still pealed as Carol went back into her room, and now there seemed a note of warning in them.

Teri was seated crosslegged on her bed, playing with the Action Man toy which she had brought him from Rome. His hair was tousled, and he was still in his pyjamas, looking very lovable and vulnerable, so that Carol couldn't resist pulling him into her arms and giving an assortment of those kisses from his babyhood.

'You want me to marry your Uncle Rudi, don't you, darling?' she asked. 'You really want to stay here on the island with him?'

'If you do, Cally,' he said, giving her a solemn look. 'He's different from those others—'

'What do you mean, Buster?'

'Those other men who look at you.' The boy put a hand against her cheek. 'You know, Cally.'

'My silly boy—'

'I'm not silly.' His fingers caught at her thick braid. 'Zio Rudi is different from them because he doesn't speak to me as if I'm in his way. He helped me to catch a real live fish and he took the hook out so its mouth didn't bleed, and I had it for nursery supper when you were away buying your dresses. It was cooked with tomatoes and I ate every bit.'

'Bones and all?' She grinned at him. 'You're happier with your own kin, and that's one good thing about all this.'

'Better than the Aunts,' he muttered, and sat his

163

Action Man on the motor-cycle and sidecar, once again losing himself in that world of childish imagination that Carol envied. How she wished she could close her mind to reality, but there was no chance of it, because when the maid brought in her breakfast tray there was a package on it beside the silver coffee pot, from the *signor baróne*, the girl told her, with that half-curious smile that everyone seems to give a bride on her wedding morning.

'*Grazie.*' Carol moved the package about in her fingers and delayed opening it until she had fortified herself with a strong cup of coffee and a *brioche*. She knew that he had sent her an item of jewellery and he would expect her to wear it at the ceremony that should be a holy and tender ritual between two people who saw no way to be happy unless they were joined in the sacred bonds of matrimony.

Her fingers were unsteady as she opened the jewel-case, and she could feel her heart beating in her throat as she stared at the lovely knot brooch composed of rubies and pearls. The gems and the gold were intricately woven together with a pendant in which a large single ruby glowed like a drop of heart's blood.

The tiger rubies, which the bride of each successive *baróne* was dowered with as a matter of course rather than the indulgence of a man who wanted his future wife to feel cherished beyond all other women. The brooch seemed to Carol to signify passion and tears, and she would wear it on the lapel of her blue wedding dress, so simple in design and yet made of the purest silk and like no other dress she had owned in her life.

Gena came to her room at eleven o'clock in order to help her get ready. Teri went off with Flavia, who would look after him during the course of the wedding and the celebration that would follow. Buffet tables and barbecues had been set up in the patios of the *palazzo*, and Carol could hear the guests arriving even as Gena helped her with her coiffure and drew from its box the wide-brimmed hat that she had chosen to wear, to the brim of which was attached a single silk rose.

At last she was ready and Gena stood back to give her a long and rather critical look. 'Yes,' she murmured, 'you were not only wise to choose blue for your dress, but you were cunning. That colour and that material are perfect on you – my brother will find you beautiful, and I'm glad about that. Everyone will think you quite stunning and people will say again that Rudi hasn't lost his touch when it comes to choosing a woman.

'Oh hell,' a look of pain crossed Gena's face, 'I wish he still had his own fabulous looks. There was no one – no other man to hold a candle to him! You might have thought Vince a good-looking specimen, but he never had Rudi's look of pride and power. Why he won't have surgery on his face I'll never know. It could be done. In America there are some wizards at that kind of thing, but he's so darned obstinate and endures those fearful scars. Can you bear them, Carol? Especially when he kisses you!'

'Strangely enough,' Carol's fingers played with the ruby pendant of his brooch, 'I sometimes don't even notice them. His pride and power are still the greater part of him, for the way we look is transient, isn't it?'

'Maybe it is,' Gena said drily, 'but all the same it's nice for a girl to be pretty, and I bet you can't look in that mirror and say you aren't glad that you look good enough for a man to eat. I quite envy your creamy English skin and the mystery of your blue eyes shaded by the brim of that romantic hat, and I'm frankly delighted that Rudi has a dish like you to enjoy – even if Vince did have first bite of the apple.'

Carol winced. 'No one would take you for a subtle Latin,' she said. 'You use American phrases as if born to them.'

'My dear girl, I've known too many Americans not to have absorbed some of their ways of speaking and thinking. Does it shock you that I'm such a liberated Latin woman?'

'I don't sit in judgment on people, Gena. I'm no angel myself.' No, thought Carol, I'm a barefaced liar and a fraud, and I'm already scared stiff that the *baróne* is going to find out about me.

Gena stared at her, as if seeing a hint of this fear in her face. 'You look as they painted the gothic angels,' she said, 'as if pursued by a secret devil. That ruby brooch is perfect against the silk of your dress; tears and kisses, eh?'

'Marriage is made of them.' Carol's fingers crept to the pendant of the brooch yet again, a sure sign that she was nervous. She'd be glad when it was all over and she was committed to the *baróne* for better or worse.

'Rudi won't be the same type of lover as Vince, but I think you realize it, don't you, Carol? There's no boy in him; he's all man.'

166

'Yes, I know.' Carol said it with a catch of her breath. 'That's why his scars don't matter.'

'You must be terribly in love with him!' Gena widened her eyes as if with a sense of shock. 'Did you know how you felt about him? My dear, you look quite white and stunned, and I'd better get you a glass of champagne and a chicken sandwich. We don't want you passing out at the altar.'

Gena left the room for a few minutes and Carol heard her speaking to someone. She guessed it was Saul, and she was right, for it was he who brought the tray with three brimming glasses on it, and a plate of sandwiches.

'Hi there!' He smiled at Carol as he came into her room. 'Say, you really look a blue angel, don't you? If all brides look as good as you do, then I might give up being a bachelor.' He held out the tray to Carol, while Gena gave a scoffing laugh.

'I don't think you're the marrying type, Saul.' She took her glass of champagne and gave him a mocking look. 'Some are like the hummingbird and they have this insatiable urge to sip nectar from a variety of flowers. My brother Vince had your kind of disposition, and look what he did to Carol.'

Saul glanced again at Carol and he raised his glass to her. 'Carol doesn't look too much of a wreck to me,' he drawled. 'Her nectar looks almost undisturbed from where I'm standing.'

Gena shot a look at Carol. 'It must be those fair looks,' she said. 'They give her that illusion of being a mere girl on the threshold of experience, but there's a bouncing boy of five to prove that Carol isn't a virginal innocent. All the same, *viva la rosa*. It's quite an asset, my dear, to look as if you've been coming to bloom behind a hedge of thorns, and that only Rudi has really dared to pluck you free of them.'

Carol sipped her champagne with a desperate, inward urge to find some measure of courage. Gena and Saul didn't mean any harm in speaking in this way, for it was the conversation of their kind of world. They were sophisticates who believed in being unconventional. That a girl should have a baby from a bigamous marriage didn't shock them, but they'd be less understanding of a girl who took on the illegitimate child of her bigamous husband and passed him off as her own. They'd regard that kind of behaviour as outrageously quixotic, and think her a bit of a fool.

She didn't really care what they thought – there was only one person whose opinion mattered, and when the moment came for her to proceed to the chapel to join him, her head swam from nerves and champagne (a sandwich would have stuck in her throat). Her fingers clenched the small bouquet of rare white orchids with a shadow of violet-blue on their curled-in petals, nested in sprigs of green fern. She felt she was killing the flowers as her nerves were killing her. Her heart beat intolerably fast as she walked along the aisle of the crowded chapel, so filled with people and flowers that it was like a scented hothouse. The colours in the peaked windows swam in front of her eyes, and then she felt a hand on her wrist, lean fingers pressing against her rapid pulse, and she looked upwards into tawny eyes and they seemed to guess at all she was feeling, and though he didn't smile she felt strangely reassured.

He drew her to his side and an excited sort of gasp seemed to emerge in concert from the crowded pews. It had been accepted for a long time that the *baróne* wouldn't marry on account of his disfigurement, caused as everyone knew by a woman. But today he stood at the altar with a girl in blue, and there was a perceptible air of drama to this marriage. No one was prepared to believe that this pretty creature was marrying the *padrone*, so tall, stern and fearfully scarred, because she had given her heart to him. There was more to it than that! The whispers ran back and forth as the white-robed priest appeared, his prayer book in hand. There was the boy – the brother's son whom this slim, fair, trembling girl had brought to the *isola*. It was for the child's sake that these two took their vows today, and everyone knew it.

Most of the ceremony was conducted in Latin, and Carol went through it in a kind of dream, there beside Rudolph in a pearl-grey suit of impeccable styling, possessed, she felt, of a quality of emotion held in steel bands. With a hand as steady as a rock he held hers and slid on to her finger the wide gold band chased with a Florentine motif of lily-flowers – symbol of love, and yet no more than a striking design on the ring that sealed their bargain. Teri was now his son . . . the *palazzo* was now her home.

Her own fingers shook uncontrollably as she took the masculine ring from the prayer book, and as she slid it on to Rudolph's finger her skin in contact with his felt as if it were receiving an electrical charge. The priest locked their hands together with his ... they were man and wife and the racking ritual was over at last.

As this final moment came the guests watched avidly ... would the *baróne* kiss his bride in front of them and how would she react, this foreign girl who was now their *padroncita*?

His arm slid firm and strong around her waist and he held her against him as he brought his dark face down to hers ... such a pale face, blue-shadowed by the wide brim of her hat, her deep blue eyes fixed upon the twisted lips.

That sense of drama was so heightened in the chapel, filled with islanders to its very doors, that a total silence fell as the bride suddenly pressed to her bridegroom and gave him her lips without protest or any outward sign of trepidation. At the same time her ringed hand touched his scarred cheek, and somewhere in the packed chapel a woman gave a choked sob.

'Bless you for that moment,' Gena said afterwards to Carol. 'It was the perfect gesture, for everyone was quite certain that you were scared out of your wits. My dear, there were moments when your voice could hardly be heard, but actions speak louder than words and it was really quite moving when you put your hand to Rudi's face. Oh, what a day! My head is spinning from all that wine and music. Teri enjoyed himself, didn't he? Dashing about with those other kids and looking every bit as Italian as they are. He doesn't resemble you, but I guess that's how it is when someone so fair has a baby with a man so dark.'

Gena turned from the *salotto* window and gave Carol a frankly curious look. 'Do you plan to give Rudi any children?' she asked.

Carol flushed deeply, not so much at the question but at what it implied in reference to the *baróne*. He had spoken of a marriage in name only, but Carol couldn't see how it was going to work. Already her personal belongings had been moved into the wing of the *palazzo* used exclusively by Rudolph, and Flavia had agreed to sleep in the room next to Teri's so he wouldn't feel too abandoned by Carol's departure. He was a precocious child who knew that a husband and wife slept in adjoining rooms, and he hadn't sulked when Carol had explained to him that she was now expected to sleep in her husband's apartment. He had taken to his uncle, and grown fond of Flavia, so there was no problem there.

The problem lay in Carol's own heart ... she was disturbed by the man she had married, and common sense told her that a man and a woman couldn't live on the edge of intimacy without being aware of each other. A marriage of pure formality could only work if they lived in separate parts of the house, but he wanted their relationship to look as normal as possible; too proud a man, and too much an Italian, to want it whispered about that he never laid hands on his attractive bride.

'*Che sarà, sarà,*' she said in answer to Gena's question. 'I've already learned that we don't really plan things for ourselves, but have to swim with the tide that catches hold of us.'

'You're being evasive,' Gena said shrewdly. 'I don't think you really know what Rudi wants of you, and much as I love him there's a forbidding pride to him that makes me stop at asking personal questions. I won't probe, Carol, so there's no need to look cornered. You and Rudi have entered into a state of privacy which excludes even a fond sister, but I'll wish you good luck in your marriage. It's quite an undertaking when someone marries a Falcone.'

They moved out into the hall after that and said good night. The last guest had drifted away an hour ago and now the *palazzo* was strangely quiet. The *baróne* had gone out into the grounds to smoke a cigar, and Carol hadn't seen anything of Bedelia for some time. As she stood alone in the hall, Gena having gone upstairs to bed, Carol looked around her and tried to believe that she was now the mistress of all this. She had become part of the history of this house, for no matter what happened privately between her and Rudolph, it was now recorded that she was his wife and her name had been entered in the huge, silver-bound recording book of the family.

She drifted from one portrait to another on the high walls and studied the faces of other Falcone brides. Mostly they had been Italians, with here and there the fairer face of some European woman. On one or two of the women she recognized the tiger rubies, and it was a startling thought that she now wore jewellery which had once adorned that austere-looking Latin with her hair in Victorian ringlets.

Suddenly she tensed and felt that she was being

watched by living eyes that made her turn sharply to look. Bedelia was standing silently in one of the embrasures of the hall, and she smiled when she saw that she had startled Carol.

'Nervous on your wedding night?' she mocked. 'After that pretty demonstration in the chapel one would suppose that you couldn't wait to get into Rudolph's arms. But I knew you were acting! I could have told those sentimental fools the truth about you, that you would do anything to get your hands on the lands and the title for that brat of yours. You would even endure his lovemaking for that, and one look at your face tonight is enough to show that it will be an endurance test. In the dark you will have to pretend that you are with Vincenzo – I believe that quite a few women act out this kind of fantasy in order to survive the lovemaking of a man they don't really fancy. Yes, that is what I advise you to do, close your eyes and make believe that you are kissing the handsome face of my husband – as you kissed it when he was alive, his long lashes against your skin, and the very tip of his finger parting your lips to his. The perfect lover, wasn't he?'

Bedelia drew nearer to Carol as she said this, and there was the faintest rustle of silk about her body, the faintest drift of musky perfume.

She was like a serpent, Carol thought wildly, slithering across the mosaic floor with a hissing sound, her tongue flickering with venom on this night when like all the others she believed that the *baróne* was going to consummate his marriage.

A tide of anger and dislike swept through her and

173

she just had to retaliate and make this bitter woman squirm in her own venom.

'I daresay Rudolph is an equally perfect lover,' she rejoined. 'Are you envious of me, Bedelia? Would you like to change places when he takes me in his arms and makes me his woman?'

'Change places with you?' Bedelia's voice rose in the quietness of the hall. 'You are welcome to have that devilish face close to yours, and those twisted lips on your body. If I didn't hate you I might pity you for having to give yourself to him. He won't be a tender lover! A woman did that to his face and he'll always feel the need to get his own back on other women, and you're the one who's vulnerable. You're now his private property, on his very own island, where he makes the laws.'

Vindictive words with an awful ring of truth in them, but even as they had their effect on Carol she flung up her head and defied anyone to see the fear that knocked at her heart. No one knew themselves, or the extent of their own passions, and Carol would be at his mercy when the door of his apartment closed behind them tonight. They were to share adjoining bedrooms and there was no knowing what memories, what pain it might trigger off when he found himself alone with her, her long fair hair let down for the night.

'Because you're vindictive,' Carol said, 'you take it for granted that everyone else is. Rudolph knows that I want security for Teri, and I'm deeply grateful to him for providing it.'

'So out of gratitude you'll give yourself to him, eh?'

Bedelia gave a laugh that was like claws scraping across silk. 'Your demon lover – why, it's like something out of one of those old melodramas, when for the sake of her family the girl sacrificed herself to a man who really frightened the heart out of her. Do you think I can't see it in your face, you little fool? You're as white as those flowers you carried to your wedding – did he provide the orchids? You know their meaning, don't you? *I await your favours.*

'Of course he does.' Bedelia ran her eyes all over Carol's slim figure. 'You've sold yourself to the devil and you'll have to pay the price.'

'Oh, stop it!' Carol could feel the edginess of her nerves – this was all she had needed, a confrontation with Bedelia to round off a day of sheer bravado on her part. Walking arm in arm with Rudolph from the chapel, the guests following beneath the flowered archways to where the decorated tables were piled with food and drink. There in front of everyone they had drunk their wedding wine, and those white orchids had been tossed into the air for one of the single girls to catch. The music had played and she had danced with her bridegroom. The smile had been fixed to her face until the muscles of her mouth had ached with tension.

Slowly the day had drawn to a close and a sort of peace had drifted into the air along with the fragrant coolness of the night.

Now that tentative peace had vanished and a new sort of tension had Carol in its grip.

'I'm going to my room!' She turned and made for the branch of the stairs that led to her old room. Remembrance stabbed and as she halted at the foot of the stairs she heard Bedelia laugh.

'Wishful thinking, dear,' there was infinite scorn in the Italian woman's voice. 'You go to *his* bed tonight.'

'You can go to hell!' Carol flung at her, and with flying skirts she dashed up the other flight of stairs and walked in the direction of Rudolph's suite as if she were going to the gallows, head high and features white as marble, feeling as if at any minute her legs would give way beneath her.

She opened the door of the suite, where there was a master bedroom and bath, a smaller bedroom fitted out for Carol, and a *salottino* with armchairs, an elegant writing-table and several book cabinets.

There was an air of luxury and style, and a subtle aroma of the tobacco he smoked. Carol opened a door which she thought led into her own bedroom, but instead she found herself in Rudolph's room. She stared at the bed where his black silk robe and pyjamas lay dark against the bedcover . . . a large bed, with carved posts soaring into the shadows of the high ceiling.

And it was there by his bed that her legs went suddenly nerveless so that she had to drop to the bed or find herself on the floor. A wave of weakness swept over her and the bravado which had kept her going all day was like sand ebbing from a rag doll. She lay there motionless, feeling the silk coverlet beneath the grip of her hand, seeing the rubies wink and gleam against the gold of her wedding ring.

She knew when the door opened, but the carpet silenced the sound of his approach. He bent over her and she felt his breath against her neck.

'So the little sacrifice awaits her demon lover,' he murmured. 'Well, my dear, if you want to pay the devil, then I'm perfectly willing to accept payment – a rather sweet one, at that.'

As he spoke his hand slid down Carol's spine and she shivered from pure emotion. The very words he used made her realize that he had caught part of that conversation with Bedelia, and she just about found the strength to turn over and face him, so she might read his eyes and try to gauge how dangerous his mood might be.

CHAPTER SEVEN

WHEN he saw the way she was looking at him, his lips gave a mocking twist.

'That is why you came in here, eh?' His eyes wandered over her face, a heaviness to his eyelids so that his lashes screened their gold to a sultry duskiness. 'That's why I find you on my bed so invitingly?'

'No—' She attempted to sit up, but his hands closed upon her shoulders and she was borne back against the silk bedspread. 'I – I mistook your room for mine—'

'With my robe and pyjamas to hand?' he mocked. 'Come, don't lose your nerve now you have come to me in this way. I assure you I'm not averse to changing the terms of our bargain if it will ease your mind to repay me for giving your child the legal right to my name and fortune.'

'Oh, you won't understand—' Carol fought her feeling of weakness, but even when her vitality was at its best she was no match for his strength, and quite deliberately he was removing the pin that secured her hair and as it tumbled around his fingers they twined themselves in its glossy strands and he held her to the bed – his prisoner of a passion she could see smouldering in his eyes.

'Pale and lovely as those orchids, and a little mysterious, aren't you, *mia*? I do indeed await your favours—'

'You were listening,' she accused. 'You heard what Bedelia said to me and now you're putting your own interpretation upon her remarks.'

'I admit it, my dear. I was about to come in from the garden after a most enjoyable smoke when I caught the sound of raised voices in the hall. I paused in the shadows and I heard you taunt Bedelia and ask if she was envious that tonight I would hold you in my arms and make you my woman. Followed by that I come to my room and find you stretched upon my bed so provocatively.'

As he spoke he forcibly took her left hand and carried it to his scarred cheek. 'Today in the chapel you touched my face in front of everyone, but like Bedelia I believe that you were acting your part to perfection. Now the show is over and tonight is a reality.'

Carol saw from his face that he meant every word, and beneath her hand she could feel the agitated movement of a tiny muscle in his jaw. Instantly her eyes filled with the fear that haunted her . . . the fear that he would find out that she had lied to him from the moment she had walked into the *palazzo*.

'I thought you were a man of your word,' she gasped. 'Y-you promised me a marriage in name only – you said there would be nothing between us but the legal formalities.'

'I meant what I said, but you are the one who has altered those terms by being here in my room, here on my bed. What did you think, that you could tease the poor beast with your beauty and then run away?'

He studied her intently and that tiny muscle throbbed

against her fingers. He leaned a little closer to her and very deliberately he traced the outlines of her pleading mouth with the very tip of his finger.

'What did you say to Bedelia, that you thought I might be as expert as my brother in the fine art of lovemaking? Shall we find out, *donna mia*? Shall I make you forget that there was ever another man in your arms?

'Please—' Taunted to the verge of panic, Carol began to struggle with him, desperate in case he learn the one thing that would reveal her as a liar and a fraud – that she had never known Vincenzo as a lover, or carried his child in her body.

'You'll regret this,' she half-sobbed, trying to turn aside her head as he forced his lips upon hers and her words of appeal were stifled by his mouth. As he felt her open lips against his, his arms tightened about her slim body and she felt the rush of his warm breath across her skin, the pressure of his lips against her throat.

'Rudi – don't!' In a sort of despair she slumped into a sudden stillness that might fool him into thinking she had fainted, but he only laughed softly, tauntingly against her ear, and there was a ripping sound of silk as he stripped her in the way of the Romans when they brought the Sabine women to their war tents. The shock of it went through her like a knife . . . she thought she screamed, but it was a distant sound and her lips were too locked by his to have given that shrill and fear-filled scream. It had to be in her mind, and then she knew that it wasn't, for he suddenly wrenched away from her and sprang to his feet. She lay there staring up at him, and he was as tensed as a tiger, his black hair in disarray, the pupils of his eyes blazing dark and almost blotting out the golden irises.

Abruptly it came again, and even as Carol struggled into a sitting position, dragging her hair around her, the door of the bedroom burst open and Gena came running into the room. Her face was ashen and she was in her nightdress.

'Rudi – Rudi,' she came to him and clutched at him, 'there's a fire! The east wing is burning and the children are there! The children – Teri and Flavia!'

It was a nightmare – it had to be. Carol stared in horror as her husband gripped his sister by the shoulders and gave her a shake.

'What are you saying, Gena?' Carol knew from the shaken sound of his voice that he was still half dazed by the stormy scene he had shared with her. She could still feel his touch on her skin, and her lips still ached from the kiss from which he had wrenched himself away. At any other time she would have been cruelly embarrassed to have been found like this, even if the man were her husband. But Gena was in the grip of a fear far greater than anything Carol could have felt with regard to Rudolph. A primitive, blood-chilling terror.

'Come!' he gripped his sister's hand and they made for the open door, where he paused but a second to fling a command at Carol. 'Get something on and go down to the hall. Hurry!'

They were gone, and Carol lost not a moment in obeying him. She scrambled off the bed, kicked her torn dress out of the way and grabbed at the black silk robe. She put it on and tied it tightly with the cord, hastening all the time from the suite, hearing again those terrified words of Gena's.

Fire in the east wing where the children slept! Fire, that most dreadful of all hazards that could face human beings! Scorching, devouring, and utterly pitiless in the face of flesh and blood!

Carol ran down the stairs at such a pace that she hardly felt her feet on the ground. And all the way down she was trying not to lose control of herself – Teri – her Teri was where the fire had broken out, and she would have been there with him if Rudolph hadn't insisted on their separation. Teri – Flavia – she wanted to be with them, for they'd be so frightened.

The servants were clustered at the foot of the stairs that led to the east wing, and the *major-domo* was handing soaking wet towels to her husband, who was swiftly wrapping them around his shoulders, his throat and his head.

No! The word screamed through her mind. He was going up there, to the gallery that was already dense with smoke. He was going where the flames were, and she moved numbly to Gena's side and looked at her with a great question in her eyes. Gena had managed to get downstairs, but how was it that the boy and girl were trapped up there?

'Their door was locked and the key was missing,' Gena said, and she stood there trembling, with her bare arms wrapped around herself. 'I tried the door and called out to them, but it wouldn't budge, and the fire had been started in the playroom right next door. I – I could see the flames and I screamed and came for Rudi. He – he's going up to get them – if he can.'

How had it happened? Had a radiator got too hot and caught something alight?

Saul came quickly to Gena and he was carrying a coat, which he wrapped around her. 'I got it from one of the footmen,' he said. 'There, it will keep you warm.'

Warm! Carol was staring with agonized eyes as Rudolph went up those smoking stairs, a tall figure, half swathed in wet towels in an effort to keep the flames from overpowering him. 'He'll die,' she thought dully, 'and I shall never be able to tell him that I love him.'

A hand caught at hers – it was Gena, looking at her with eyes that suffered for her. 'He insisted on going alone – let him go, Carol, let him get the children out if he can. He isn't afraid of being burned – he's been there, right there where it hurts like hell, and if anyone can get the kids, he can!'

A convulsive shudder went all through Carol that once again her husband – her Rudi – had to face the torment of being seared as only flame and acid could sear the flesh. Still so vividly could she feel herself in his arms, struggling not against him but afraid of what he would discover when he took total possession of her – that she was a virgin bride.

Now she was bitterly sorry that such a crucial point in their lives had not been reached, and she wanted to rush up those stairs and join him, and as if Gena sensed this her fingers tightened on Carol's arm.

'Don't!' she said tersely. 'He mustn't be distracted – it will be bad enough for him if the children are lost, but you must stay here with us!'

'Not here!' Saul took hold of both of them. 'Come along, everyone!' He raised his voice. 'Outside! It will be safer out in the open!'

Even as they went out into the courtyard the smoke was writhing across the hall and the smell of burning timber was strong.

'Can the fire be fought?' Carol asked, through trembling lips. 'Has the island some sort of fire service?'

'Of course,' said Gena, 'and they're on their way.'

'Look!' Someone pointed up at the windows of the burning wing, and they saw in horror the living flame curling up the window frames, and suddenly beyond the flames a figure could be seen, a sort of nightmare thing that had to be made of wax and cardboard, for it was alight, flaring like an effigy, and moving, moving towards those windows from which the glass suddenly flew, lethal and glittering in the firelight, falling like darts through the air as that human torch sank out of sight.

There was a terrible, stunned silence, and then Gena gave a groan and buried her face against Saul.

'It was a woman,' he said, in a shocked voice. 'I saw her long hair burning!'

'It was Bedelia,' Gena whispered. 'I knew she was going mad – I just knew it! Rudi should have sent her away before she had the chance to do something like this. The wedding today finally unbalanced her—'

Carol swayed where she stood, feeling sickened,

hung in a web of cold shock. She was chilled to the bone even as they heard the fierce crackling of the flames, eating away at the walls and the furnishings, ruthlessly destroying part of the *palazzo*. She more than anyone should have guessed that Bedelia would have her own back on Rudolph for marrying the girl who was the supposed mother of Vincenzo's child. That for Bedelia had been the final blow to her pride, and this fire was the horrifying result. She had locked Teri in with Flavia, and then gone into the playroom to set light to the toys. In so doing she had trapped herself, for fire was an even more unpredictable enemy than a woman driven mad by love she had lost more than five years ago. A love stolen by Carol, so she died believing.

'Oh, Cynara,' Carol thought, the wetness of tears on her cheeks, 'this time because of you I may lose a real man.'

She could taste the ashes on her lips, and as she stood there in her husband's black robe her unbound hair attracted the glint of the fire and was like a cape of gold silk about her shoulders. She couldn't take her eyes from the upper part of the east wing, where the flames had spread until each window was a frame for them. She heard the clamour of the firemen as they arrived, but not a scrap of hope revived in her heart. She felt certain she would never see Rudi again, and that if she did if it would be as the blackened ember of a man, the golden eyes burned away ... oh no, she choked and swayed as a figure suddenly emerged from the house into the courtyard. It was a figure black with soot, tattered and torn, seared and grinning so that the bone-white teeth were agleam against the blackened skin. He lurched out into the open, one child clinging around his neck, and the other safely locked in his arms.

'Sweet, sweet air!' It was the most jubilant cry Carol had ever heard in her life, and then she was alive again and running to him, stumbling over the water hoses, treading in the puddles, crying out his name from the very depths of her heart. Saul took the children from him, and Rudi stood there dragging deep gulps of air into his lungs. Carol stared up dreamlike into that dirty face, the gold eyes dazzling her through the smoky mask.

'Y-you look as if you've come down the chimney,' she said, and she stroked his arm, his shoulder where his shirt had burned away, making sure he was still in one piece. His jacket was gone, wrapped around Teri, who was coughing and calling her name. She caught him to her, and she still couldn't take her eyes from her husband's face. 'I'm eating him,' she thought, shamelessly, 'eating him in front of everyone, and I don't care a damn. I love him! Oh God, how I love him!'

'Thank you,' she whispered.

'You are welcome, madam.' He looked right into her eyes, and it was as if they were the only two people in all the chaotic world, in that dazzling moment as bricks and timbers fell flying through the air and the night was lit by a thousand sparks. Those sparks were in her blood itself, and because *he* was alive, she too was alive as never before.

'Santa, my dear,' he smiled his twisted smile, 'bringing you a pair of presents – the children we love even if they're not our own.'

He said it with an infinite softness, for her ears alone, and his smile crept, growing more and more wicked.

She felt Teri's clinging arms, and she saw in Rudi's eyes his teasing knowledge of a lot of things. Then he moved away from her to speak to the fire chief, and because not yet had the moment come for him to explain, Carol turned to the others, to Flavia in the circle of Gena's arm, the terror slowly seeping from her young face.

'Dear, dear Rudi,' the tears glittered in Gena's eyes. 'Don't you have to love him – don't you see what he is, the sort who walks through hell for those he cares about.'

Carol had no speech left in her, her throat locked as she held Teri and felt him little and live against her. She saw Saul glance at Gena and there was a faintly cynical smile in his green eyes. He wanted Rudi's sister, Carol could see that, but he also knew that he was going to have a devil of a job convincing her that he had his good points even if he couldn't compete with the powerful charisma of her tall, scarred brother – once upon a time the handsomest man in Italy.

The dawn came, spilling over the shell of the east wing. Carol stirred sleepily in Rudi's arms and pressed her lips to his scars, counting each one as if it were a gem.

'Shameless hussy,' he murmured, 'daring to tell me all those lies. Aren't you ashamed of yourself?'

'Not any more.' She curled close into his arms and

187

she felt that nothing, no moment could ever be more heavenly than this, to wake a bride in the arms of a most beloved man, and find him so alive and warm and human.

'It was wicked of you to lead me on,' she smiled against his chest, feeling the crisp hair against her face. 'I might have guessed that a shrewd Italian wouldn't make a business deal without finding out all the angles. So you had me checked on, did you?'

'Up to the hilt.' As he spoke his hand moved under her swathe of hair, moving up her spine until she wiggled and gasped with laughter.

'Don't, Rudi, I'm ticklish!'

'Yes, aren't you?' His mouth came down against the side of her neck and he kissed her with a slow, knowing humour. 'Delicious little liar, I ought to beat your rump for not telling me the truth. Do you think I'd have thrown *you* out on your ear? I took one look at you and wished to heaven I didn't look a ghoul—'

'Don't!' This time she made a different sound, and she flung her hand quickly across his lips. 'You're the most marvellous man in the world and I love you so much I don't know what to do with it—'

'Shall I tell you?' he breathed. 'Oh, shall I tell you, my little witch, who watched me go up those stairs to the fire as if at any moment you would dash after me. I prayed you wouldn't. I could face the flames for myself, but not for you – beautiful girl, sweet virgin, giving to me those first sweet cries. *Mia adorata*, I thank you for loving this face of mine.'

'All of you,' she gasped. 'Every sinew of you, Rudi –

but what if my sister Cynara ever wants her boy—?'

'To hell with Cynara, I'll kill her first!' And his lips took Carol's and he took her once again to that heaven reserved for true lovers. No more doubts, no more lies . . he knew; she could feel how much he knew that he was the only man she had ever loved *like this*.

And one day, when her love for him had taken away all his pain, he would tell her about that other woman . . . the one who had thrown the vitriol as if to say, 'If I can't have you, then I shall make sure that no other woman ever wants you!'

Only it hadn't worked out like that, for love moves in mysterious ways, and with the eyes of the heart had Carol learned to love the master of Falconetti.

Mills & Boon
Best Seller Romances

The very best of Mills & Boon
brought back for those of you
who missed reading them when they
were first published.
There are three other Best Seller Romances
for you to collect this month.

SHOW ME
by Janet Dailey

It was seven years since Tanya had seen her husband Jake, but their
young son needed a father and now she had asked him to come home.
But even in the circumstances she was not prepared for the hostility
and suspicion with which Jake treated her. Was it worth trying to
save their marriage?

BELOVED RAKE
by Anne Hampson

Serra Costalos had married Dirk Morgan because she couldn't face
the thought of the arranged Greek marriage that was all she could
expect from life. Dirk had married her because he needed a wife who
wouldn't make a nuisance of herself. But neither of them got what
they expected!

TAKE WHAT YOU WANT
by Anne Mather

Sophie was only a teenager, but she knew she would never love, had
never loved, anyone but her stepbrother Robert. But her whole
family, including Robert, disapproved, and hoped she would get over
the feeling. Were they right – or was Sophie?

If you have difficulty in obtaining any of these books through
your local paperback retailer, write to:

Mills & Boon Reader Service
P.O. Box 236, Thornton Road, Croydon, Surrey, CR9 3RU

One of the best things in life is...FREE

We're sure you have enjoyed this Mills & Boon romance. So we'd like you to know about the other titles we offer. A world of variety in romance. From the best authors in the world of romance.

The Mills & Boon Reader Service Catalogue lists all the romances that are currently in stock. So if there are any titles that you cannot obtain or have missed in the past, you can get the romances you want DELIVERED DIRECT to your home.

The Reader Service Catalogue is free. Simply send the coupon – or drop us a line asking for the catalogue.

Post to: Mills & Boon Reader Service, P.O. Box 236, Thornton Road, Croydon, Surrey CR9 3RU, England.

*Please note: READERS IN SOUTH AFRICA please write to: Mills & Boon Ltd., P.O. Box 1872, Johannesburg 2000, S. Africa.

Please send me my FREE copy of the Mills & Boon Reader Service Catalogue.

NAME (Mrs/Miss) _____ EP1

ADDRESS _____

_____

COUNTY/COUNTRY_____ POST/ZIP CODE_____

BLOCK LETTERS, PLEASE

Mills & Boon
the rose of romance